The Man From Belize
Steven Kobrin

Granada Hills, CA
"Select books for selective readers"

For information, contact: henrygraypub2022@gmail.com

Publisher's Cataloging-in-Publication Data

Names: Kobrin, Steven, 1971—.
Title: The man from Belize / Steven Kobrin.
Description: Granada Hills, CA : Henry Gray Publishing, 2023. | Series: The man from Belize ; book 1. |
Identifiers: LCCN 2023903432 | ISBN 9781960415028 (pbk.) | ISBN 9781960415035 (ebook)
Subjects: LCSH: Assassins -- Fiction. | Mercenaries -- Fiction. | Spies -- Fiction. | Surgeons -- Fiction. | Belize -- Fiction. | Mérida (Mexico) -- Fiction. | Yucatán Peninsula -- Fiction. | BISAC: FICTION / Action & Adventure. | FICTION / Thrillers / Espionage. | FICTION / Thrillers / Suspense
Classification: LCC PS3611.O53 M36 2023 | DDC 813 K67—dc23
LC record available at https://lccn.loc.gov/2023903432

Library of Congress Control Number: 2023903432

Cover illustration by Bruce Scivally, © 2023 Bruce Scivally.

Made in the United States of America.

Published by Henry Gray Publishing, P.O. Box 33832,
Granada Hills, California 91394.

For more information or to join our mailing list,

visit HenryGrayPublishing.com

The Man From Belize

1

LOS ANGELES

A brisk, balmy afternoon. Perfect weather for a ball game. The stadium was mostly filled. Some openings in the nosebleed seats, otherwise it was a full house.

Art Jensen was a fan. He loved the game. A fit, appealing man in his forties, nothing gave him a bigger thrill than to watch his home team play like champions. This was not one of those days. The feeling in the air wasn't quite right. He knew there was a presence at the stadium. Something or someone that didn't belong. It was cool out yet beads of sweat ran down his temples.

Tanya, his beautiful, much younger wife, couldn't help but notice that he was distracted. "What's wrong?" she asked.

He glanced over at her nervously, reluctant to acknowledge that anything was amiss. "Sorry?" he said.

"It's like 70 degrees outside, and you're sweating aa if it were summer in the Yucatan."

Art managed a slight but nervous smile.

"I'm fine. I just can't believe this game."

Tanya chuckled demurely. She leaned over to whisper in his ear, "They might actually win this one."

With sweat covering his face, he looked into the eyes of his companion. He couldn't help but think how lucky he was to have found her.

They tenderly gave each other a small kiss.

Tanya reached into her purse, pulled out some tissue and handed it to Art. "Just dab yourself with this. Stay cool."

"Thanks." Art began to wipe his brow, feeling slightly embarrassed.

Something was off. Art sensed some anomaly ahead of him, across the way in the section near right field. He gazed at the seats with a cold, hard stare, striving to tune out everything else around him. Then the sound captured his attention. As loud as anything going on at the stadium. The cocking of a sniper's rifle. Despite the din of the crowd, he heard it clear as a bell.

The beads of sweat began to roll more profusely, and then...

The bat smashed the ball like a thunderclap, echoing across the stadium. The sound was particularly sharp behind home plate, where Art and Tanya were seated.

The whole stadium rose to their feet to clap and cheer, including Tanya. The batter scored a double streamed right down center field. But Art remained in his seat, the only one behind home plate who didn't rise to see the team get on base.

The crowd was now anxious. It had suddenly become anybody's game. As the cheers gradually began to subside, the fans took their seats. But Art's focus was no longer on the action on the field.

"Honey, get me a drink," said Tanya. Art, staring out towards left field, didn't respond. So she repeated, "Art?"

He suddenly snapped out of it. "Sorry?"

"Could you please get me a drink?"

"Oh yeah, sure. Sprite?" Tanya smiled and nodded.

Art flagged down the vendor. Bought a couple of sodas. The vendor was a happy man with a sincere smile and pleasant manner. The total was seven bucks. Art handed him a ten spot, saying "Keep the change."

He took his seat again, trying his best to focus on the game. After all, his team looked as though it actually stood a chance.

His cell phone buzzed, on vibrate. He reached into the breast pocket of his coat and retrieved it. It was an older style flip phone; Art Jensen wasn't a fan of technology. He preferred to keep things simple.

"Hello?"

No response.

Is anyone there?" Silence.

After a pause, the call went dead. Art tapped the "Recents" button and glanced at the phone curiously. It was an unknown number.

Then his attention was once again riveted by the unmistakable sound of the cocking of a sniper's rifle. To him, it seemed to echo from every corner of the stadium, yet no one else seemed to hear it—only him.

He looked straight ahead towards center field. Then, as if out of a nightmare, a single shot permeated the air.

Art bolted from his seat. The rest of the spectators in his section remained planted, the ones nearest him gazing at him curiously. Tanya grabbed his hand and gave it a tug, signaling for him to sit back down.

"You didn't hear that?" he asked.

Tanya was puzzled more by his tone than the question. "Hear what?"

Art was baffled. How could she not have heard the shot? Maybe he was losing it. Hearing things.

"You mean did I hear how this crowd is going nuts because your team may actually pull off a fuckin' miracle and win one?" she laughed. "Yeah, I heard that."

Tanya could always lighten his mood. They smiled to each other. He began to rub his brow.

"Are you sure you're alright?"

Art looked at her, his face suddenly showing concern. "I, uh... I think I need to take a walk." He rose from his seat.

As he stepped across his lovely wife, she once again reached for his hand and gave it a tender squeeze. "Hey..."

Art glanced back at her.

"Love you," she said. And she meant it. Theirs was a truly special bond, and they both knew it.

He winked at her and continued toward the aisle. She kept her eyes on him, watching him. She loved his strong physique and undeniably masculine presence. Women in the surrounding seats also turned to gaze at him as he strode up to the back section of the stadium.

The home team scored another hit. This one went back deep into left field. A home run. The crowd went completely insane. Art Jensen paused on the steps and joined in the applause. As he turned to continue to the exit door, a little blonde girl accidentally dropped her large soda. It instantly covered the step she and her father were standing on and began trickling down the steps below. It almost splashed over Art's shoes but he dodged it just in time. The girl's father, embarrassed by his daughter's clumsiness, glanced at Art, saying, "Sorry about that."

"No worries," Art responded, continuing past them as the father flagged down an usher to alert them to the mess.

Art weaved his way around several fans, some heading for the bathrooms, others meandering towards the concession stands or searching for souvenir vendors. Art suddenly found them suffocating. He just wanted to find a quiet spot where he could be alone and clear his head.

Eventually, he reached the entrance of the stadium. It was much quieter there. He could actually hear himself think. He paused for a moment. His pensive mood was not easily broken despite the overriding pandemonium at the game.

He pulled out his phone and stared at it.

Then he made a call. His determination was undeniable. Art Jensen was looking for closure. The phone rang on the other end. Once. Twice. Three times.

Then a click as someone answered. "This is Jensen," he said, trying to be discreet. "I think I have a tail...Of course I did...Look, I didn't find the fucking thing!!" His voice was rising. He looked around to make sure he wasn't stirring up too much commotion.

"Just listen to me, please. Listen...I want to come in. I have information that would be useful to you...Who?"

A look of deep regret heightened his moody, scornful eyes.

"As far as I know, yes he is. For some time now...almost ten years. That's right. One of the heads of the facility. He's made quite a name for himself...But look, I just want to come in and be done with this, all right? I'll give you everything I have and believe me this shit matters!!! You want me to come in! You need me to come in!!"

There was an extended response by the person on the other end of the phone. It seemed to bring a great sense of calm and security to Art, as though it were exactly what he wanted to hear. "When? Fine...And then what?"

A confident smile spread across his handsome face. Now he felt better. Things were starting to look up.

"You can count on me," he said. "Yes sir, I'll be there... No, thank you. Bye."

Art ended the call, relieved, feeling like a tremendous weight had been lifted off his shoulders. Now he could relax. Breathe easier. Now...he could go back inside and enjoy watching his favorite team actually win one.

Yes, indeed. Things were looking up.

He walked with more confidence and authority as he moved back towards the section where Tanya was waiting. Then the sound rang out like a storm at midnight. Another base hit.

The crowd again leapt to their feet. It was the bottom of the ninth. Some people were already beginning to clear out—the ones who didn't want to get trapped in heavy traffic leaving the stadium—so it was a bit more packed in the back section as Art pushed through the fans beginning to clog the exits.

Among the people exiting was a strange-looking man in his twenties with aviator glasses and a grey leather coat, also trying to navigate past the sea of people. But as he did so, he eased closer and closer to Art.

Art was about a half-dozen steps above his row—aisle 11—when the strange-looking man stumbled as though bumped from behind and fell against him. It was a rough hit, abrupt and easily felt, colliding with Art's chest. Art flinched, winded. Seemingly embarrassed, the man gave a quick, apologetic wave and moved on, swiftly disappearing into the departing fans.

Wincing and clutching his midsection, his eyes beginning to flutter, Art turned to get a better look at the man with the glasses and grey coat. No sign of him at all. He was gone. Art continued down the aisle towards his seat, but he felt off, increasingly weak. He moved very gingerly down each step, grabbing tightly at his waist.

The man with the aviator glasses reached the exit door. Before pushing it open he retracted a curved blade back inside his jacket sleeve. He already knew what Art would very soon discover—the blow was fatal. As he'd bumped into Art Jensen, the man had sliced quickly and deeply into his femoral artery. And now he was dissolving into the throngs heading for their vehicles in the crowded parking lot. Soon he would be gone.

His mission was complete. He had dispatched the target.

Art found his way back to his seat and slumped into it.

Tanya was bubbling with enthusiasm. "Man on third," she reported excitedly, bringing him up to speed. "One more hit and we've won."

Her eyes riveted to the game, she hadn't noticed the color draining from his face, or the sweat now flowing in rivulets from his temples and brow. But she turned her head when she heard his erratic breathing, and saw that he was fighting to keep his eyes open. "Art, are you sick? What is it? What's wrong?"

A few rows behind, an older woman looked down at the spilled soda which hadn't yet been cleaned up. As the dark, syrupy cola slowly flowed down each step, there was a noticeable red streak running through it. She put on her glasses to get a better look.

Art turned to his wife for what he already knew was the last time and then...

A base hit! The man on third dashed towards home. It was the winning run the home team needed. The game was theirs! The crowd rose to their feet and cheered wildly.

Art tried to say something to Tanya, his visage growing increasingly pale. "I..."

In that moment, his head slumped forward. Tanya noticed his hand still tightly clutching his thigh, and saw the immense pool of bright red forming around his jeans. She pulled his coat away from his waist and was aghast and terrified at the sight before her. A small crimson lake had formed, increasing as blood pulsated from the femoral artery where the blade had penetrated.

He was bleeding out. And it was already too late. Art Jensen was dead.

Tanya screamed. Her tears flowed freely.

Art was the love of her life, and now he had been ripped away from her.

The crowd around and behind Art and Tanya Jensen was oblivious to the tragedy which lay right before them. Tanya tenderly held her husband's head in her hands and cradled him close to her chest.

It was over.

As was the game.

The home team won.

2

KILAUEA, HAWAII

Kilauea is an active shield volcano in the Hawaiian Islands. Located along the southeastern shore of the big island of Hawaii, the volcano is around 250,000 years old. It emerged above sea level almost 100,000 years ago. In keeping with its volatile and inherently unpredictable nature, Kilauea is also one of the most active volcanoes on Earth.

A destination for curious tourists since the mid-1840's, it was now host to a variety of geologists, world travelers, and thrill seekers looking for a way to indulge and explore within the vast reaches, unprecedented beauty, and undoubted savagery of Mother Nature. And one never knew when there could be an eruptive episode at Kilauea. It could happen... at any given moment. But in recent years, the malevolent mountain had been relatively calm.

This particular day was unusual. The sun shone quietly across the lush, vertiginous landscape sending a heatwave that was mildly suppressed by scattered clouds and the veiled threat of a gathering storm. Weather was like the migrating tropical birds of paradise scattered across the floral terrain— their patterns were forever changing.

A lone figure of a man stood along the tourist-friendly ridge of the mountainside overlooking Kilauea. There were a few scattered hikers, carrying backpacks and a variety of photographic equipment, making their way across to the other side of the ridge.

Gavin Weller was a player. He loved the game of life. And he was always up to face a challenge no matter how severe the risk or the cost. As he approached his early sixties, he resembled a sleek, grey fox with his full head of salt and pepper hair. His deep tan and youthful complexion belied his actual age. Dressed in casual blue jeans and an Ocean Pacific short sleeved button-down shirt, he looked on the surface to be an ordinary local, just another resident of the islands. But Gavin Weller was far from that. He had a commanding presence and an effortless, immediate sense of authority about him when he spoke. Gavin Weller was no local. Utterly corrupt and viciously ruthless, he was like a human embodiment of Kilauea, calm on the surface, broiling inside, volatile and inherently unpredictable.

Weller was head of a top-secret organization known only as The Sandbox.

About twenty-five years ago, The Sandbox had begun as a means of having an elite, covert organization for dispensing with the more nefarious criminals in the world, particularly those who posed a considerable threat to national security. Known only to its members, the organization always operated deep in yhe shadows. They were never spoken about in the private sector, and they certainly never received any publicity or press. But as time passed, its members became fearful for their own lives and those of their families. Allegiances were dismantled, and in certain parts of the world, trade secrets were exposed.

For all intents and purposes, The Sandbox had been dissolved a decade ago. But over the course of the past three years, some of its key members began to disappear and die under mysterious circumstances. These were sanctioned hits—contracts authorized by one man, the only man who could give the green light to killings of this nature: Gavin Weller.

But for Weller, today was not a day for killing. He inhaled the ocean air, ruminating calmly about the world and its potential. The natural beauty of the surroundings was completely overwhelming, with verdant, green mountains and rainbow-colored fauna surrounded by the stunning volcanic site. Paradise on Earth, a veritable Eden, with Weller its seductive serpent.

The silence was swiftly and suddenly broken by the droning of a gradually descending helicopter approaching the ridge of the mountainside adjacent to the volcano. The helicopter slowly and carefully landed along the grassy hillside. A lone male passenger exited the side door. He tapped the chopper to indicate that he was out and they could leave. The menacing, mechanical bird ascended to the sky and began to fly northbound back to the mainland of the big island.

A confident smile marked Weller's face as he walked towards the other man. His name was Gil Losado. A company man who had been with The Sandbox for about twelve years, trained as a contract killer at first, Losado eventually moved his way up the ranks through consummate skill and peerless bravado, catching both the eye and favors of Weller. In time he became his right-hand man, organizing contracts around the world rather than actually executing them himself. But that was fine by Losado. He was a smooth, ambitious piece of work. Patience and servitude were his gifts, and he knew that the keys to the kingdom would one day be his ultimate prize. So he was alright with being at Weller's beck and call at any given moment. In Losado's mind, he would one day reach the proverbial light at the end of the tunnel.

"Gavin!" called Losado as he waved and approached Weller with a faintly exhausted smile. Weller waved and signaled for Losado to come over. They shook hands with habitual form and routine. For them, this was just another day at the office.

"I'm glad you made it," said Gavin with his typically jovial demeanor.

"Good to see you again, Gavin."

"Gil, have you ever been to Hawaii?"

"No, sir. I can't say that I have. But I must say..." Gil saw a rock formation shaped almost like a table a few feet behind

Gavin Weller. A few tall drinks were perched upon it. The arrangement seemed very curious. "…This is a most unusual place to meet."

Gavin gave Gil a skeptical look. "You don't approve?"

A slight rumbling across the ridge echoed in the distance, emanating from the ominous yet dormant volcano. Gil looked intimidated but coolly tried to hide it. Weller remained completely calm.

"Not at all, sir. This is...lovely."

A slight smile formed across Weller's lips as he sensed the obvious trepidation in Losado's demeanor. "Don't concern yourself, Gil. Stress is a killer."

Losado swiftly looked over his shoulder and towards the tip of the volcano.

"We're perfectly safe, Gil," said Weller. "The volcano is dormant this time of year. There hasn't been a serious eruption in... longer than I can remember."

"Of course, sir," said Losado.

"And besides, you don't really think I would arrange for us to have a casual business meeting and put both of our lives at risk in the process... do you? Gil tentatively shook his head. "We are humanitarians, Gil."

Losado mustered a nervous smile. "Indeed we are, Mr. Weller."

Weller turned away from Losado and took the ice-cold drinks resting atop the jagged rock formation. He handed one of them to Losado. "Mint Julep," he said.

Losado took the drink and raised it politely in a toast. Weller took a sip, savoring the crisp flavor. The echo of distant thunder sounded behind them followed closely by a brief, shimmering veil of lightning which crackled across the overcast sky.

"So what's the update?" asked Weller.

"The L.A. contract is complete," said Losado.

"How did it go?"

"Smooth as silk."

"And our contact?"

"Already taken care of," Losado whispered in a hushed, sinuous manner.

"That's what I like to hear. You know, we're getting closer."

"We are indeed, Mr. Weller."

"As soon as we deal with that little scenario in the Caribbean, we'll have control of all the ports. Nothing will move in or through those waterways without us allowing it to happen. With our base of operations relocated in that area, we'll have diplomatic immunity from everyone and everything."

Losado raised his glass to make a formal toast. "To the future, Gavin."

They clinked their Mint Juleps together.

"Not quite, Gil. Not until we handle our last bit of business... Our man in Belize should be seen as top priority. Who do you have on it?"

"The specialist we recently deployed to Monte Carlo to handle the Marseilles Affair."

Weller thought for a moment. "The Viper? What's his status?"

"Hasn't made confirmation yet. But he's competing in the blackjack tournament at the casino, so you might say he's part of the inner circle."

"The security on Mr. Bonnot will be extremely tight."

"Not to worry, Gavin. Just remember that where there is a will, there is a way."

"And The Viper always finds a way."

"Exactly," said Losado as he smiled wickedly. Losado finished his drink and took a step forward, looking at Weller in a concerned manner. "Gavin, there is just one thing I'm curious about. Is there some reason why..."

"The others will be taken care of in due time. Let's just say that I believe the man in Belize to be in possession of certain... privileged information."

Thunder shattered the skies again. It was a bit louder and a menacing streak of lightning followed.

"Understood. I'll advise The Viper. But sir..." Weller raised a curious eyebrow. Losado continued, "Given the circumstances, do we still proceed with everything as originally conceived?"

The Machiavellian scheme that Weller had devised was gradually coming together. And although the scale of his ultimate plans were vast and far-reaching, he firmly felt in his Orwellian mind that once revealed, his true agenda would benefit the world in the long run. He managed a slight smile and raised his glass.

"We do."

3

MONTE CARLO

Among the glittering gambling meccas of Europe, the Casino De Monte Carlo was the undisputed crown jewel, the absolute reference point for all major Blackjack players, who enjoyed its wide variety of prestigious tables.

Inside, the casino was truly a masterpiece to behold, with magnificent statues and fountains adorning the lobby and the outer shell of the building, attracting the world's high-rollers in droves. This was where the top players came to win and the elites came to lose. If you had money to burn and you liked to place high bets while surrounded by beautiful people, this was definitely the place to be.

The casino was frequented by an international array of men and women dressed to the nines, the men looking like figures from the pages of GQ while the women were so ravishing that they all must have been actresses or models in this lifetime or another. The ambiance was the absolute definition of high class, sizzling with an undercurrent of decadence and sin. People came to gamble as much as they came for the five-star cuisine. They also came to grab a stiff drink as much as they came to find a fabulous fuck.

This day was even more exciting than usual—the VIP room was hosting a Blackjack tournament. It was a two-person game with a ten thousand dollar buy-in. One-on-one was the order of the day and the current winner was a minor local celebrity, Pierre Bonnot. Today he was on a winning streak like never before. He had already defeated nine players; ten was the limit and then a new pair needed to take the table; those were the house rules.

Bonnot, in his mid-thirties, had skills that extended far beyond the gaming tables. A stylish, sophisticated man of the world, he was also a drug dealer, white slaver, and gunrunner. Blackjack was his game of choice and he played to win, usually in the company of well-armed bodyguards.

This evening was no exception. He had his muscle flanking him on both sides—two hulking, intimidating hoods in shades and dark suits.

A man in a white tuxedo sauntered through the front entrance of the casino. He could have been a Latin James Bond. Indeed, his suit was identical to the one worn by Sean Connery in the opening scene of what he considered to be the best James Bond picture ever made.

The man's name was Ignacio. Mid-thirties, of Spanish background and with an extremely handsome face, he turned women on simply by looking at them. He had that kind of charisma. Standing at six feet two inches, his dark hair pulled back into a short pony tail, Ignacio radiated class and elegance. But he did not speak. Not because he deliberately made that choice, but because he was a deaf-mute.

Henri was the manager of the casino. Friendly and extremely affable, he was friends with Ignacio and greeted him warmly as soon as he saw him. He knew how to sign and this is how they communicated.

Henri asked him if he was here on business.

Ignacio said he was visiting friends in Nice and it was strictly pleasure.

Henri asked how long he was planning on staying in Monte Carlo. Ignacio replied he had already been there three days. He stopped by the casino just for a quick round of Blackjack and then he would need to catch a flight. Henri walked him to the cashier to get some chips. 30,000 Euros worth. Ignacio's credit here was fine.

Henri personally escorted him to the VIP lounge, where the Blackjack tournament was in progress. All eyes turned to Henri and Ignacio as they entered.

Bonnot glanced at them both like a predator sizing up his prey. "Who's your friend, Henri?"

"His name is Ignacio, and he'd love to play a game."

"Is that so?"

Ignacio could read lips when looking directly at the person speaking to him. He smiled politely as he nodded affirmatively.

"10,000 buy-in, Ignacio," said Bonnot. "Is that alright with you?"

Ignacio laid €10,000 in chips on the table.

Bonnot liked what he saw and pointed for Ignacio to have a seat. The game was on.

The newcomer attracted attention. Elegantly dressed men and women soon surrounded the table. Immersed in the game. Mesmerized by the action. Studying the players' every movement.

The first game passed fairly quickly. Two cards in and Ignacio hit 23 while Bonnot held at 18. Game over.

The second game was a nail-biter. Longer plays and smaller cards being dealt. By the fourth card dealt, Ignacio was at 19. He stood. Now it was Bonnot's turn.

Bonnot signaled the croupier to deal him another card.

He examined the cards, maintaining a proverbial poker face throughout. A gorgeous lavender-eyed blonde in a red cocktail dress stood right behind Bonnot. She bit her lip as she noticed his hand.

The hood to the right of Bonnot smiled curtly, anticipating the next move.

Ignacio signaled Henri to have the bartender send over two drinks. A couple of Tom Collins.

The onlookers were in a dire state of suspense. Dying to know what kind of hand Bonnot was prepared to lay down. It was the last move. He examined Ignacio thoroughly, looking at him from top to bottom. Prepared to extend his last play as long as he could.

"I know you're here to play, Ignacio," he said drily. "But I'm sure you also came to win."

Ignacio stared straight at him, completely aware of what Bonnot just said. He maintained a calm, steely stillness.

"And it was a very nice game you played, Ignacio. A good hand. But I'm afraid... it wasn't good enough."

With that, he laid the cards down on the table. A perfect hand of 21. Two eights and a five.

The onlookers gasped and applauded. Bonnot leaned back in his chair, extending his arms out and gesturing a move of resigned victory. Of course he expected to win.

As the applause subsided, Ignacio placed some cash on the table, then removed a small bottle of hand lotion from his pocket. With his hands out of sight below the tabletop, he snapped open the cap of the bottle and rubbed the liquid into his hands thoroughly, until it dissolved. He then put the bottle back into his pocket.

The bartender brought over the drinks and set them down. Ignacio nodded at the cash on the table—a generous tip. The bartender took it, nodding his thanks.

As Ignacio stood, the bystanders began to peel away and veer off. Ignacio offered one of the drink to Bonnot with a slight bow. Bonnot was amused yet impressed by this noble gesture even in the face of defeat.

"You're offering me a drink?

Ignacio smiled politely and nodded.

Bonnot took the drink from his hand. Staring into Ignacio's eyes, he raised the glass. "Ignacio, if you win as gracefully as you lose, then I must say this makes you a true gentleman. I thank you."

Ignacio appreciated the remark and gave a curt nod.

Bonnot took a swig of the drink.

Ignacio turned away and left the table, flanked by Henri.

Bonnot watched them exit and said to the bodyguards behind him, "Interesting man."

Henri and Ignacio moved from the VIP room and into the lobby, where a constant parade of well-dressed people were coming in and out of the casino. They looked at each other as friends would, standing by the foyer, preparing to say goodbye.

After a moment of conversing in sign language to each other, a bellman approached Henri to get a signature for one of the casino guests.

"Pardon me, sir," said the bellman, "but Mr. Vandenberg was looking for credit at the Roulette Wheel."

Henri turned away from Ignacio to address the bellman. He took the pen and signed the credit slip, saying, "No problem. Mr. Vandenberg is one of our most reliable guests."

"Thank you, sir." The bellman headed back to the VIP room.

When Henri turned back to continue his goodbyes to Ignacio, his friend was already gone, having disappeared like a phantom in the night. Henri shrugged and walked back to the casino. His friend would be back soon enough.

Outside the Casino De Monte Carlo, Ignacio approached a sleek grey Porsche Panamera. He was parked on the street by the main highway, so he wouldn't have to bother with the parking valets. He entered his car, closed the door, settled in the driver's seat, and then opened the glove compartment to remove a pair of tweezers. He examined each of his hands and delicately began to peel away what appeared to be the top layer of skin from each hand. Once fully removed the layers looked like a pair of thin latex gloves formed to fit each of his hands perfectly. As the layers dangled off the tweezers, they looked like dead skin. Careful not to touch any part of them, Ignacio opened his door and dropped the two artificial skin gloves right through the slatted grill over which he was parked. It led directly to the sewer.

Meanwhile, inside the casino's VIP room, Bonnot, having finished his drink, had just lain down a hand and humiliated another victim. But then a strange feeling consumed him. He instantly became short of breath, like he was being squeezed by a python. His face went pale. He stood, shakily, clutching his heart.

No one in the lounge knew what to do. They were too shocked. Sudden agonized paroxysms at the gaming tables simply weren't done.

Within seconds, Bonnot's eyes rolled up into the back of his head. He fell to the ground like a ton of bricks. One of his bodyguards placed an ear to Bonnot's chest. Then he grabbed Bonnot's wrist, feeling for a pulse. Nothing. The bodyguard sadly shook his head. And like that Pierre Bonnot was dead from sudden cardiac arrest.

Ignacio checked his watch. It was 11:30 in the evening. There were sirens in the distance, coming closer, but Ignacio could not hear them. But he did notice their flashing lights as they pulled up the drive to the entrance.

He smiled, satisfied. Of course he knew exactly why they were there. He knew Pierre Bonnot had died. He knew the glass from his drink had been coated with a toxic fluid that killed him within minutes. If the fluid made contact with unprotected skin, it was absolutely lethal to the touch. This was why Ignacio wore the protective gloves when he handed Bonnot the drink. Indeed, Bonnot had come there to win but this evening he had lost everything. Without knowing it would happen, he had become the next in a long line of victims to fall prey to the international assassin known as The Viper.

As the sirens of emergency units continued to sound off in the distance approaching the casino, the Porsche sped up the highway on the way to the airport.

Ignacio had a plane to catch.

4

BELIZE

Having been appointed Head Surgeon of the Cardiovascular department of the Karl Huesner Memorial Hospital, Kent Stirling took both his work and his patients very seriously. He truly cared about each and every one of them, and his genuine warmth and compassion extended to his friends and colleagues, making him one of the hospital's most respected surgeons. Physically speaking, Stirling cut an impressive figure, standing over six feet tall with a superb physique. With an American father and Mexican mother, his look was distinctive and unusual. His features were sharp with a unique profile and deep-set eyes, and an engaging smile that put both staff and patients at ease as he made his usual rounds, offering kind words to everyone.

The head nurse on call was Martha Dominguez, a stern woman of about sixty with a heart of gold, whose genuine high regard for Stirling was mutual. A native of Mexico City, she had a fairly strong knowledge of English, which she kept sharpened by speaking in that tongue to Stirling, who was fluent in both English and Spanish.

"Good morning, Martha," said Stirling, approaching her.

"Dr. Stirling, so nice to see you this morning. I wasn't expecting you until next Thursday. I thought you were off to the Yucatan today."

"I am. My flight leaves in a couple of hours. But I wanted to stop by just so I could make the morning rounds."

"How nice," said Martha.

They approached the elevator. Stirling was on his way to catch his flight to Merida, Yucatan.

"Martha, I have a favor to ask you."

"Yes, of course."

"Mr. Quintero in room 17 is scheduled for a quadruple bypass a week from today. He was complaining about some lower back pain when I visited with him."

"Was he having the shortness of breath issue?"

"Just some discomfort. But please do me a favor and simply keep him comfortable. And mind his intake of beef and pork where the meals are concerned."

"He won't like it."

Stirling entered the elevator. "Just use that impeccable charm of yours." Martha was always swayed by Stirling's little compliments. "Oh, and please let Dr. Tamayo know that I should be back next Thursday afternoon, and to inform Refugio of Quintero's surgery next Friday."

"Yes, I will," she responded. As the elevator door slowly closed, she added, "Have a wonderful trip!" Stirling winked and waved goodbye to her.

Minutes later, Stirling—having changed into blue jeans and a beige silk shirt, sat in the backseat of a cab cruising steadily along the highway en route to the airport. Staring out the window, he admired the natural beauty of his surroundings. It was a stunning day; the bright rays of the sun reflected delicately on the sea, causing the waves to sparkle like diamonds. There was nothing in the world quite like the aquamarine water of the Caribbean Sea along the coastline of Belize.

The cab driver was a local transplant from Mexico, rather than a native Belizean. But that was typical of Belize, which was a true melting pot with cultural influences ranging from Creole to Mayan to French to Mexican. Stirling noticed the driver's I.D. badge on the dashboard. His name was Ramon Valdivia, and he was a small man with a deep tan and hooded eyes. Seventies disco music emanated at a moderate volume from the radio.

Stirling addressed him in Spanish. "Ramon?"

The driver lowered the radio so they could speak without raising their voices. "Yes, sir?"

"You wouldn't happen to know what the weather forecast is for Merida, would you?"

"As a matter of fact, I do. My sister lives down there. We just spoke last night. She was telling me a storm passed through yesterday afternoon but by the evening it was back to being clear and about 80 degrees."

"Sounds beautiful. Are you from Merida? I don't really hear the accent."

"Actually no, I'm from Guadalajara."

"I love Guadalajara. Beautiful city."

"Thank you, sir."

"And how do you like Belize?"

"Aaaahhh... Belize is amazing. I would never leave here, sir. This place is truly paradise. A little piece of heaven on earth."

"It certainly is," agreed Stirling with a smile as he again turned his head to look out the window, watching beachcombers cavort in the tranquil sea.

"And what takes you to Merida, sir?" asked Ramon. "Is it business or pleasure?"

Stirling thought for a moment. "A bit of both, I suppose."

The cab continued its smooth journey up the highway, eventually arriving at the outskirts of Philip S.W. Goldson International Airport.

Tropic Air Flight 118 bound for Merida looked as though it was going to be full. The tarmac had well over 100 people lining up to board the plane, including Stirling, who was just reaching the top of the airstair, his carry-on bag in tow. As he entered the plane, a very attractive flight attendant at the entry door directed him to his seat with an elegant hand gesture and a lovely smile.

Down below at the foot of the airstair, about half the passengers were still in the process of boarding the plane. A single older woman with floral pants, excessive jewelry, and entirely too much make-up examined herself in her compact, as though it were her sacred duty to look as flawless as possible at all moments of the day.

About half a step in front of her stood a man dressed in a casual linen suit. As she closed her compact, she couldn't help but notice his beautiful Movado watch. "I bought my husband a watch just like that one for our 35th anniversary," she said. "He loved it."

The man said nothing, keeping his eyes forward. The woman found this off-putting, and more than a little rude, but she was not one to be put off easily. She tried another conversational gambit: "Did you enjoy Belize?"

Now he cast a glance at her, and simply smiled. Her face cast a reflection in the lenses of his aviator glasses. But rather than respond, he simply turned his attention back to the airstair, continuing the slow trek forward. The woman abruptly turned away from him and muttered to herself, "What an asshole."

She moved forward past an elderly passenger who was struggling with his roll-on luggage and cut in line in front of him so boldly that no one dared challenge her. Disgusting woman, thought Ignacio.

The skies were clear for the crew and passengers of Tropic Air Flight 118 to Merida that morning. And their flight was about to be joined by a very special passenger, because the silent man in the linen suit with the Movado watch was Ignacio.

The Viper.

5

Flight 118 was almost at maximum capacity, filling up with an array of people from all walks of life and all parts of the world. Among the last passengers to enter the crowded cabin was Ignacio, with a handful of other on-boarding passengers cramming in behind him.

As Ignacio made his way down the aisle, he gave only a passing glance to Kent Stirling, taking note that Stirling was in the window seat of row 9, seeming completely relaxed, eyes closed, wearing headphones and catching up on much-needed rest.

A couple of obnoxious, drunk college men in their early twenties stumbled into Ignacio from behind, pushing him forward. He didn't bother to look back and acknowledge them; the last thing he wanted was to make a scene that would draw attention to himself.

He arrived at his aisle seat at row 14 and saw that the center seat next to him was already occupied by the woman who had complimented his watch back on the tarmac. She gave him a perplexed look as he sat down.

"You again?" she asked with a note of disdain.

Ignacio, buckling his seatbelt, was unaware of her remark and did not respond. The woman thought he was being purposely aloof. Asshole.

Lilia, an attractive flight attendant, came down the aisle doing a head count. She suddenly stopped when she arrived at row number 14, having noticed that the woman with the overdone makeup had her overstuffed carry-on bag protruding from underneath the seat in front of her.

Lilia pegged the woman as American just by her haughty demeanor, so instead of her native Spanish, she addressed her in polite, slightly-accented English.

"Excuse me, Miss?"

"Chambers. Evelyn Chambers. Is something wrong?"

Lilia motioned at her bag. "I'm sorry, but your carry-on item can't be sticking out that far."

"It doesn't bother me."

"I understand, Miss..."

"It's Mrs.," said Evelyn curtly. "And it fits on other airlines. Maybe if you didn't make your planes so cramped..."

"Sorry, Mrs. Chambers," said Lilia, cutting off her harangue, "it's just that it's a safety hazard. I'm afraid we're going to have to put it with the luggage below or else see if we can get it into the overhead compartment."

Caught in the middle of this contretemps, Ignacio didn't need to read Lilia's lips to know what was happening—it was obvious from her body language. Deciding to remain neutral, he looked straight ahead with a slightly bemused expression.

With some effort in the cramped space, Evelyn tugged the heavy case out from underneath the seat and pulled it up onto her lap. Now breathing heavily, she looked over at Ignacio, who had begun casually thumbing through an in-flight magazine. Evelyn shifted her attention to Lilia, giving her an exasperated look and gesturing silently if she could ask Ignacio to put the bag in the overhead.

Lilia put her hand on Ignacio's shoulder. He glanced up at her, reading her lips as she asked, "Sir, I'm so sorry to bother you, but the lady seated next to you was wondering if you could place her bag in the overhead compartment."

Ignacio smiled and gave her a nod to acknowledge that it was fine. Unbuckling and standing up, he gently took the heavy bag from Evelyn's lap as Lilia opened the overhead.

He took the opportunity to steal a glance at Stirling before hefting the bag up to his shoulder. Whatever was inside—a pressure cooker? Bowling balls?—shifted, and he almost lost his grip on it.

"Be careful with that!" Evelyn commanded.

And now Ignacio saw that the overhead bin was almost completely filled with other pieces of luggage. This was going to be a more involved task than he expected. He'd have to remove other pieces of luggage in order to accommodate her one piece comfortably. Setting her bag down on his seat with exaggerated carefulness, he set to work as quick as possible removing and rearranging the bags in the overhead, with Lilia assisting.

With his back now to Stirling, he didn't notice Esther, a brunette flight attendant with a pixie-ish face and petite figure, come in behind the last boarding passengers and rush to Stirling's side, out of breath, as though she'd been running.

She shook him lightly in order to wake him. "Dr. Stirling?" His eyes snapped open, and he recognized Esther's familiar face, having flown this route many times previously. Seeing the anxious worry in her eyes, he removed his headphones quickly.

"Yes?"

"Dr. Stirling, I'm so sorry to bother you, but we have an airport employee who's short of breath and holding his chest. He's having terrible pains and his arm is hurting as well."

"Left arm?" he asked. Esther nodded. "Where's he seated?"

"Oh, he's not on the plane, he's in the terminal."

Stirling rose quickly to his feet. "Alright, Esther," he said, gathering his belongings. "Could you please arrange for me to be placed on the next flight to Merida?"

Esther smiled knowingly. "I've already put in the request."

Grabbing his briefcase, Stirling followed Esther out the boarding gate. As they exited, a passenger who'd just about given up on getting a stand-by seat came aboard to take Stirling's place.

Ignacio had practically emptied the overhead bin to make room to shove Evelyn's bag inside it, and had then proceeded to position other bags around it until the compartment was full. As he was placing the remaining luggage into the next overhead bin, he saw the new passenger taking the window seat of row 9. Stirling was gone. With determined purpose and cat-like grace, Ignacio quickly finished his task and snapped the overhead bins shut. Ignoring obnoxious Evenlyn's grateful smile, he yanked his briefcase from beneath his seat and began making his way to the entry door.

Lilia stopped him. "Sorry, Sir," she said. "The cabin door's closed. We're about to start taxiing."

Ignacio was not thrilled with this turn of events. But, it seemed, every mission had some unpredictable element that couldn't be controlled, not even by him. So Stirling was staying behind while he traveled to Merida.

He sat back down in his seat. Put his briefcase back underneath the one in front of him. Buckled his seatbelt.He felt a slight tremor as the jet's engines powered up.

Did Stirling get some warning? Was he aware of Ignacio's presence? Or was there some other reason he was called away, and he'd be on the next flight?

If he was still coming to Merida, Ignacio would be waiting for him.

His thoughts were interrupted by Evelyn giving him a pat on the arm. "That was very kind," she said. "Thank you for helping."

He responded with a polite, formal nod. She was beginning to catch on that he was mute, or deaf, or both. But she no longer thought he was an asshole. Not at all. He was nice, polite, with a kind heart. She could tell—she'd always been a good judge of character.

The jet shook as it roared down the runway and took to the sky. As it climbed, the passenger in the window seat

of row 9 craned his head to look out at the sparkling sea below. Ignacio's jaw muscles flinched, his eyes narrowed, his
rage simmered.

Stupid woman! This was all her fault. He glared at her.
She gave him an insipid smile. He went back to his in-flight
magazine, ignoring her, and considered offering her one of
his special cocktails.

6

MERIDA, YUCATAN, MEXICO

In the heart of the colony of Itzimna, within the infamous section of colonial Merida known as the Paseo De Montejo, was a busy boulevard known as the Prolongacion Montejo. Nestled among its regional shops and cafes stood the Banamex Bank, where Stirling had just completed a transaction and was now exiting back into the bustling pedestrians.

Though he considered himself casually dressed, he was still more stylish than the locals, some of whom cast suspicious glances at the stranger as he walked along holding a leather pouch. Waiting on the corner for a crossing light to change, he smiled at an attractive young Yucatan woman, who blushed in return. Then, he heard a familiar voice call, "Doctor K!"

He looked around to find a Mexican with deep blue eyes who was a foot shorter than Stirling but had twice his girth, who greeted him with a gap-toothed smile. "Fernando!" said Stirling, shaking his friend's hand. "Were you following me?"

"Not today, Doctor K. But I can if you want me to."

The light changed. Stirling crossed the street, Fernando keeping pace at his side. The two men had known each other for several years; Fernando was a gossip who seemed to always know what was going on in the city, both in the open and underground, and wasn't shy about selling that information to the highest bidder. Some would call him an informer, some would call him a snitch. He saw himself as a businessman, whose stock in trade was information.

As they walked at a rapid clip up the Paseo Montejo, Stirling asked his friend, "So what's the good word, Nando?"

"What you see is what you get. I just got paid today and I am feeling great! Ready to buy a yacht just like yours," said Fernando in his heavily-accented English, made almost unintelligible by how fast he spoke.

Stirling replied, "Well invite me for a spin once you have her."

"Si, both you and your beautiful girlfriend. What was her name?"

"Irina."

"Right. That's it. Irina. And how is she?"

"She's doing great. As a matter of fact, I'm just on my way to meet her for dinner."

"Well, give her a big kiss for me, and give her a good you-know-what like you mean it."

Stirling laughed in spite of himself. He was almost at his car, a new champagne-colored BMW 750IL. He clicked his key fob, and the car beeped as the doors unlocked.

Fernando's eyes swept over the automobile from front to back. "You still driving this piece of shit?" he said, pretending to be unimpressed.

"I'm afraid so," said Stirling, opening the door and tossing the leather pouch into the passenger seat. "You need a lift anywhere?"

"No, no, I'm fine," said Fernando. "My limo's going to pick me up any minute now."

"Ah, but of course," said Stirling. "Take care of yourself, Nando. See you soon."

As Stirling went to get into the car, Fernando stepped forward, saying, "Doctor K! Wait a moment..." Fernando fidgeted nervously, unsure of whether he should divulge a secret to his old friend.

Pausing beside his open car door, Stirling asked, "What is it?"

Fernando exhaled a reluctant sigh, shoulders drooping, and took a step closer to Stirling so he could speak quietly and still be heard over the din of traffic. "I... I just wanted you to know that I've..." He stopped, took another step forward, and blurted out, "Somebody new is... asking questions."

"About what?"

"About you."

Stirling's smile didn't break, but it suddenly went from being friendly to seeming forced. "A man in the medical field?" he asked, with a note of concern.

Fernando guffawed, Stirling's remark seeming so out of left field. "No..." he chortled. "This was no doctor."

And now Stirling's forced smile disappeared. In a steady voice, he asked, "You spoke to him yourself?"

"No. Not me. But someone I trust."

"What did this... new person ask?"

"Only if anyone in town knew anything about a Dr. Kent Stirling. As I said, I didn't speak to him myself, but I did see him."

"And?"

"He didn't look like he was from around here. He was... maybe Spanish... maybe Italian. Something foreign. Other than that, I... I know nothing else."

Stirling sensed Fernando was on the level, and even though the information was next to useless, he gave him a half-smile and said, "Thanks, Nando, I appreciate the heads up. I'll, uh... I'll be in touch."

Once again, Stirling went to get into his car, and once again was brought up short by Fernando exclaiming, "Doc!!" Stirling turned back to Fernando to see him rubbing his thumb and forefinger together, a gleam in his eye, indicating he wanted to be paid for the information, even if it had little value.

Anxious to be on his way, Stirling said, "Come by my office in Progreso tomorrow. I'll tell Olivia to have a check waiting for you."

Fernando gave him a thumbs up. "Thank you, Doctor K. I hope you and Irina have a wonderful time tonight."

"We will, Nando. And thanks again."

With a little wave that was almost like a salute, Fernando sauntered away. Stirling got into his car and closed the door. But before starting the engine, he paused, a worried look in his eyes. He'd been out of the game, under the radar, for several years now. Why this sudden interest in his whereabouts?

Restaurante Amaro was a regional favorite among the denizens of Merida. Located in the historical center near downtown, it was easy to miss from the outside, squeezed between two clothing stores, but once inside, a curved archway opened into a cozy and inviting outdoor courtyard, with wooden tables and chairs, bread served on cutting boards and main courses on platters suited to the enormous portions. The central seating area was a favorite spot for those in a romantic mood, with tables underneath a 200-year-old orchid tree frequented by hummingbirds. But the most elegant touch was Trova music, influenced by the sounds of the nearby island of Cuba, played by live musicians, or trovadores, on a little stage.

Stirling was shown to a table in the center of the courtyard. He ordered a red wine to sip as he listened to the music, casually eyeing the patrons at surrounding tables. It was a busy Friday night, with almost every table filled with couples making their plans for the weekend and enjoying the warm night air wafted about by fans positioned above to create a pleasant breeze.

Had he been tested, Stirling, after a casual glance around, would have been able to describe every person in the room in startling detail. He wasn't born with a photographic memory, but he'd been trained to have one. There once was a time when knowing what the person sitting one seat back and to the right was wearing, the color of his eyes and hair, his approximate height and weight, and any identifying marks like blemishes, scars, or tattoos could have been vital information.

And then he noticed her. Irina Contreras. She entered the courtyard and instantly locked eyes with Stirling. She was in her mid-thirties but looked ten years younger, with flawless olive-toned skin, dark brown eyes, and a long, cascading mane of ebony black hair. She stood five-feet-six-inches with a perfectly proportioned body—full, perfect breasts, heart shaped hips, and the most perfect legs Stirling had ever seen. She wore little make-up; she didn't need to hide, only to enhance.

Stirling put his wine aside and rose to greet Irina as she glided across the tiles in her form-fitting sleeveless white dress and nude-colored heels, her face lighting up with a seductive smile that warmed his heart. They embraced and kissed like new lovers, but in fact they'd been together for three years; unfortunately, his medical appointments and her work—event planning—kept them apart from each other more often than they liked. But their absences from each other stoked the burning passion that was lit when they first set eyes on each other.

Stirling pulled her seat out for her, and as she sat, their waiter, Felipe, approached the table. "Something to drink, Miss Irina?"

"Thank you, Felipe," she said. " I'll have a Cape Cod. Right away."

Stirling took his seat and admired her from across the table. "You look great," he said.

"I had a long day. The caterers for that event got pushed back with their schedule. So now we have to meet tomorrow morning just so we can go over the items, place the order, and figure out the seating arrangements."

"Still...you can't complain," said Stirling.

Irina was piqued by the remark. "How do you figure?"

Stirling took a sip of his wine and gave her a bemused look. "Irina... you're the most popular event planner in Merida. You've got people from Cancun to Veracruz seeking out your services. I don't think you're entirely in what I would call a bad place."

Felipe approached and set her Cape Cod before her. "Thank you," she said. As she sipped her much-needed drink, she pondered Stirling's remark. "True," she said. "It isn't the most important thing."

"What is?"

She slid her hand across the table to grasp his. "That we finally have some time together."

"Well…" he said softly, "Let's make the most of it."

They raised their glasses in a toast as Felipe returned to the table. "Ready to place your order?" the rotund man asked.

"Yes Felipe," said Irina. "I'll have the Pollo Yucateca and the Tortilla Soup."

Felipe turned his attention to Stirling. "And you, Dr. Stirling?"

"I'll have…the Cochinita Pibil and the Caesar Salad. Thank you, Felipe."

Felipe took their menus with a smile and retreated.

Irina sensed Stirling was in an quiet, more contemplative mood than usual. "You okay?" she asked.

"Fine," he said casually, trying to be disarming. He failed.

"Come on," she said, "what's on your mind?"

Stirling should have known better than to try to hide his feelings from Irina. They were too close, too connected, for him to be able to pull the wool over her eyes. "To be honest," he said, "the last couple of days have just been… strange."

"Why? What happened?"

"First it was my flight here from Belize. Just when I'm on the plane and ready to leave, I'm escorted off because an airport employee was in cardiac arrest."

"My God, is he alright?"

"Fit as a fiddle. Turns out it was nothing more than an anxiety attack."

"Well, thank goodness it wasn't something severe."

"Yes, but then there was today..." He seemed to be re-playing the events in his head as he spoke.

Irina leaned forward. "What about today?"

"I'm leaving the bank and suddenly Fernando stops me in the middle of the street."

"Oh, your little informer," she said with a note of amusement.

"Yes. He was cracking jokes at first like he always does, but then he said something odd."

"Which was?"

Felipe came forward with the soup and salad. Stirling instinctively went silent while he placed their food on the table very carefully.

"Thank you, Felipe," said Irina.

Stirling watched Felipe as he walked away.

"Kent?" said Irina. "What did Fernando say?"

Stirling leaned forward. "He said...there was some-one in town asking questions about me."

"What's so strange about that? Maybe he just needs a referral."

"It was pretty clear from how he said it that Fernando thought otherwise."

"Is that so?"

"And he said that while he didn't speak to the man himself, he did catch a glimpse of him..."

"And?"

"He'd never seen him before."

Irina could see that the prospect of a mystery man ask-ing about Stirling was nagging at him. But she also felt there was a simpler explanation. "That's just Nando," she said dismissively. "Probably looking for an excuse to get paid."

"You think he made it all up?"

"He's done it before."

Stirling considered what Irina said, but it just didn't feel right. "I know he's done that in the past, but this…This felt sincere."

"Oh, I'm sure he sincerely needs to pay his rent," quipped Irina, trying to allay Stirling's worries. "Honestly, Kent, you're very well-known in the medical community here. I'm sure it was just a professional inquiry of some sort."

"Maybe you're right," said Stirling, hoping it was true. He gave her hand a squeeze, lifted it, and kissed her fingers.

As if on cue, the musicians behind Stirling launched into their next set. It was a local band, Los Valientes—the Brave Ones—well-known in Merida for their mix of classic Mexican ballads and vibrant Mariachi rhythms.

"Shall we?" Irina asked Stirling. He shook his head no, but she stood, still holding his hand. Rather than embarrass her, he rose and followed her, holding hands, to a small space in front of the band. But before they began dancing, Irina leaned into the band's leader and whispered in his ear. The band leader nodded, and soon the music segued into a ballad from the early '70s that had been popularized by a Spanish singer named Nino Bravo—*Un Beso Y Una Flor*, or *A Kiss and a Flower.*

"Shall we?"

As the other diners watched, Irina and Stirling began to dance. He was wary at first, reluctant to let down his guard, but maybe the wine, or maybe the sight of her luscious body undulating in front of him, broke down his resistance. He gave himself up to the music and began to dance freely. It was, as Irina had suspected, just what he needed—moving to the music, pulling her close, feeling her warm body against his, one arm around her waist, her head resting on his shoulder—his tensions melted away.

As the song ended, the other diners politely applauded the dancing couple. Stirling thanked the band, and he
and Irina returned to their table. She'd worked her magic
on him, as only she could. The events of the day suddenly seemed of little consequence. All that mattered now was
being here, with her, and the pleasures of the night still to
come on this lovely evening in Merida, Yucatan.

7

A black Mercedes turned a corner into the exclusive section of Merida called Montecristo, just ten miles inland from the Gulf of Mexico. Montecristo was one of the more exclusive neighborhoods in Merida, a city known as the cultural capital of Yucatan, which was counted amongst the safest places to live on the entire North American continent and one of the best small cities in the world. But today, there was a viper in this Garden of Eden.

The Mercedes pulled slowly to the corner and parked.

Ignacio emerged from the car, wearing his customary aviator specs. He took his time surveying the surroundings, then approached the corner of 5th and 49th streets, where a palatial two-story mansion stood on a lot the size of half a football field. There were no neighbors to either side, those equally-large lots having remained undeveloped. Unlike the newer homes in the area, which tended toward modern architecture and had the appearance of giant shoeboxes stacked atop one another, this one was pure Spanish Villa, on a grand scale. On the outside, there was an in-ground pool and private shaded yard as well as a carport for three vehicles. The residence itself had barred windows on the lower level, and appeared to have a patio on top for sunbathing. A high fence surrounded the property, with only one remotely-operated gate providing entrance.

Kent Stirling was living well, thought Ignacio.

For now, there appeared to be no one at home. There were no cars visible, and no signs of life in the house. This was one of two residences Stirling owned in Merida; the other was his beach house in Progreso, which he also used as a private practice. Ignacio had already confirmed that Stirling had appointments there today.

He stepped to the gate, peering through the bars to get a better look at the front door. It had three locks. Even at this distance, he recognized the makes and models. Now if he could just locate the alarm system…

He didn't hear the motorcycle pull up behind him and stop, but he noticed the unmistakable shadow of a motorcycle patrolman approaching. Ignacio turned to the officer with a polite smile. The patrolman was only average height, under six foot, and stout. He walked like John Wayne in an old Western, the stalwart lawman protecting his territory as if each home were his own. "Sir," he barked, "do you live here?"

Ignacio momentarily debated if he should just snap the man's neck and be done with it, but that would hardly be considered remaining inconspicuous. Instead, he removed his glasses, the better to capture every word the patrolman said, and slid his hand into his coat pocket to remove a card. He handed it to the patrolman, who read its message:

> **I am deaf, but I can read your lips.**
> **Please enunciate clearly.**

The patrolman handed the card back to Ignacio. "Can't hear, huh?" he said, speaking more loudly and pausing between each word.

Ignacio shook his head and gestured at the gate to indicate that he'd lost his key and couldn't get inside.

"Oh!" said the patrolman. "You've locked yourself out?"

Ignacio shrugged his shoulders and gave a "silly me" smile.

"No problem," said the patrolman, practically shouting. "My brother-in-law's a locksmith. I'll call and have him come right over."

That was not the response Ignacio was looking for. This idiot's eagerness to please might be the death of him…

And it very well could have been, except for the intrusion of Eva, a petite but comely woman from the neighborhood who happened by in her Jeep. Seeing the patrolman, whom she recognized, she slowed to a stop. "Officer Dominguez," she purred, "what brings you to our lovely neck of the woods?"

Dominguez immediately shifted his attention from Ignacio to fixate on Eva, his eyes instantly taking her in from the tan legs sticking out of her khaki shorts to the freckles of her slightly bobbed nose. Ignacio could tell from the reddening of his cheeks that he was smitten with the woman.

"Miss Eva, so nice to see you. I'm just uh, you know, making sure your lovely neighborhood is free from any criminal activity."

Eva cast a glance at Ignacio. "This man doesn't look like a criminal."

Ignacio saw his chance. He smiled at Eva, gave a little nod to the patrolman, and strolled back to his Mercedes. The patrolman's attention was already elsewhere, as he continued making small talk with a woman he'd like to date, if he just had the gumption to ask. Just like John Wayne in some old movie.

Ignacio got into his car and made his getaway.

He'd seen enough.

He would come back prepared.

The port city of Progreso was a frequent stopping place for cruise lines, with its long pier and an oceanfront promenade dotted with thatched-roof restaurants to separate the tourists from their dollars. It was also the location of the Tropical Suites Hotel, the only one in Progreso with a clear view of the ocean. Though it wasn't a five-star hotel, the rooms were decent enough. What it lacked in ambiance and amenities it more than made up for with its breathtaking view of the ocean, provided you were blessed with a beach-side room.

One such room, number 305, had just been reserved by Ignacio, who entered carrying two oversized suitcases. He set the larger one on the floor at the foot of the bed and the smaller one atop it. Opening the smaller suitcase, he reached in to pull out a zippered clothing rack case. This he hung in the closet.

Shucking off his coat, he opened a sliding door and stepped onto the balcony. Down below, he could see the latest cruise ship slowly easing into the port. It was more of a floating Las Vegas resort than a ship, a booze-soaked paradise of gambling and gluttony for gringos from the U.S. looking to visit the Mayan ruins of Chichén Itzá and other nearby sites.

Ignacio breathed in the salty ocean air, and watched the sun make its slow descent into the cerulean sea.

At dusk, Ignacio made his way down to Progreso Beach and headed for Sol y Mar, a hangout and seafood place on the main drag that was a particular favorite of both the locals and the tourists lured in by the free post-meal tequila shots. Here it was always guaranteed that you could grab a tasty Margarita, an ice cold beer, an order of Ceviche or any other seafood delicacy and enjoy them while relaxing to the seaside views.

Ignacio was seated at a corner table looking out at the street, with a perfect view of the ocean beyond with its sailboats and water skiers, and the beach crowded with sunbathers.

He nursed a beer and took his time with the Surf & Turf Combo—filet mignon and crab legs. A short, pleasant waiter approached him from behind, asking. "Sir, how is everything?"

With no response from Ignacio, the waiter repeated the question. Still nothing. So he reached out and tapped

Ignacio's shoulder. Now Ignacio slowly turned his head and looked directly at the face of the waiter, who asked, "Can I get you anything else?"

Ignacio waved his hand, signaling that all was fine. The waiter smiled politely and retreated.

Retrieving a pair of binoculars from the seat next to him, Ignacio raised them to his eyes and looked out across the surf. Beyond the beachcombers and sunbathers was an impressive yacht docked by the pier. A man who looked distinctly American was cleaning around its deck.

Behind Ignacio, a new customer entered the restaurant—Heidi Aronson, a six-foot tall former model in her late thirties. Half-American and half-Argentine, she was now the owner of a prominent modeling agency located in Merida called Los Angeles de Yucatan, or the Angels of the Yucatan. And she looked like an angel herself, with her sandy blonde hair, green eyes, and glowing olive skin. She'd come to Sol y Mar on a location scout, hoping to use its colorful decorations and beach backdrop for a fashion shoot to showcase her models.

Enrique Puerto, proprietor of Sol y Mar, wasn't too keen on the idea. "Heidi, we've been through this before," he said. "This is my busy season. I have tourists and locals coming through here at all hours of the day. Your photo shoot would be a distraction."

"Enrique, are you kidding? All these beautiful women scattered around your place—you'll probably double your business. Or triple it. And everywhere the photos run, I'll put a credit—photographed at Sol y Mar. It's free publicity."

Enrique considered this for a moment. She had a point.

Sensing she was winning him over, she continued, "I promise, we won't get in the way of your customers. I just want to show off these stunning women in a stunning location, and what better is there than this?"

Her flattery was doing the trick. "Well..." sighed Enrique, "where did you have in mind to do the shoot? I mean, exactly where?"

She began to explain her concept to Enrique, of having the models photographed beginning at the bar area and then working back towards the seafront. As she walked him through it, Ignacio stood to get a better fix on the yacht with his binoculars.

They collided.

Heidi was immediately apologetic; here she was trying to convince Enrique they wouldn't get in the way of the customers and she'd literally bumped into one.

Ignacio gestured all was fine, and then looked up into her eyes. She was almost as tall as he, and seemed liked a goddess in the soft light of dusk. He had the faintest sense he'd seen her before—a movie? A TV show? Magazine cover? And she looked into his dark eyes and saw danger.

She liked danger.

And she liked his dark hair, aquiline nose, and strong chin. His were the most perfectly proportioned features she'd ever seen on a man. He could have been a model himself. But no, she'd never run into him before. Backlit by the sun reflecting off the sea, he seemed to have a glowing aura surrounding him. *He looks just like an angel,* she thought.

"I'm sorry," she said. "I didn't realize you were there."

Ignacio gave her a warm smile and a slight shrug, indicating he was fine.

Feeling a little breathless, Heidi said to the proprietor, "Enrique, dear, could you please bring me a drink? Something cold. I'm feeling a little winded."

"A mojito?" asked Enrique, getting the hint.

"That'll be fine. Thank you."

Enrique went for the drink and Heidi turned her full attention back to Ignacio.

"I'm Heidi," she said, putting out her hand.

He smiled, shook her hand, and reached into his pocket, pulling out his card. She looked at it, looked at Ignacio, and rather than being put off by his disability, seemed intrigued. This was nothing new to her; her own younger sister was hearing-impaired. She communicated this to Ignacio with sign language. His eyes widened in surprise. Who was this woman?

Continuing in sign language, she asked, "What brings you to the Yucatan?"

Ignacio signed his response: "I'm here visiting a friend and closing a business deal."

"Really?" she asked. "That sounds like fun. What business are you in?"

Ignacio hesitated. He was definitely intrigued by this woman, but he was on a mission, and it would be thoroughly unprofessional to complicate it with a fling. And above all else, Ignacio was a professional.

"I'm sorry," he signed, "but I'm late for an appointment. It was very nice to have bumped into you, Heidi."

He extended his hand.

She was taken aback. The only men who rebuffed her were the weak ones who were intimidated by her beauty and take-charge character—the ones who were scared of her. This man didn't look like he was scared of anything. And yet, he was giving her the brush-off.

She shook his hand. But she waited for him to release the handshake. And he held for just a fraction of a second too long for someone who wasn't interested. Then, abruptly pulling his hand from hers, he snatched up his binoculars and strode briskly to the door.

Enrique came to her with her mojito, chuckling. "Well," he said, "you certainly sent him away in a hurry."

"Did I?" she asked coyly. Taking a sip of her drink, she added, "He'll be back."

8

Away from Progreso's sixteen-block-long boardwalk and beach with their cruise ships and shops and tourists, nestled in a semi-private cove that was visited more by nesting pink flamingos than vacation-goers, was the beach home and private practice of Dr. Kent Stirling. He kept the place here for convenience; in addition to his practice, he was on the Board of Directors of the prestigious Star Medica Hospital in Merida, which often required his presence. On occasion, he led certain surgical procedures for special patients, those who lived their lives in the public eye but paid handsomely to have their medical treatments kept private.

On this day, he was seeing some of his regular patients. The consultations were quick and mostly routine. As he worked through them, he engaged his patients in friendly banter, keeping them at ease. They liked him, enjoyed his bedside manner, and most importantly, trusted him completely and utterly with their health.

After the last patient of the day left the office, giving Stirling a warm smile and a wave, Stirling let out a sigh of satisfaction and turned to his receptionist, Olivia Yanez, behind the front desk. An attractive dark-haired native of Merida, she was in her early thirties and always kept a bright, sunny disposition, which the patients appreciated. Stirling suspected they came as much to see her as to see him. He wasn't wrong.

His office manager as well as his personal secretary, Olivia was organized, efficient, and attentive to everyone's needs—especially Stirling's. At one time in the remote past, after she'd been in his employ for a year or so, they'd given in to their mutual attraction and become lovers. But as sometimes happens, they ultimately agreed they were better as friends. But since they couldn't bear to fully part from one another, she remained as his assistant and sometimes confidante, and kept him to his schedule more personably than any electronic calendar ever could.

"You do remember that the convention begins on Tuesday?" she asked him.

Finishing his final notes, he asked, "Where is it this year?"

"The first part's at the Hyatt Regency, and then the final receptions with the special guest speakers will be at the Fiesta Americana."

Stirling's eyebrows shot up. "Impressive."

"Aren't you conducting one of the symposiums this year?"

"Tamayo asked me to, but I haven't made up my mind yet."

"You mean you don't want to?"

"I do, but their means to an end doesn't really coincide with my agenda. They really need to focus their attention on creating better methods of recovery for elderly people who are having post-operative stress."

"So…you don't want to?" Olivia repeated.

Stirling sighed. "I just wish the board could get it right, because if they only want me to lecture on cardiovascular surgical procedures, then…I'm not interested."

"Well, whatever you decide, I'm sure Tamayo will be okay with it," she assured him.

Suddenly the barking of a dog sounded throughout the hallway, and Lola—Olivia's adorable little Silky Terrier—scampered into the office. The three-year-old had dark brown eyes and a keen sense of intuition. Besides being friendly and loving, she was unceasingly loyal and an absolutely uncanny watchdog. Stirling had a soft spot for the pet; she was like Olivia's avatar.

"Lola!" called Olivia. "Come here my little Lola!" She snapped her fingers and Lola jumped up on the reception desk and began to give Olivia little doggie besos.

"Lola," joked Stirling, "you want to be my back-up receptionist?" He petted Lola's head and scratched behind her ears.

"What do you mean, back-up?" said Olivia. "You're not getting rid of me."

"Not if I can help it," said Stirling.

They heard a man's voice call "Hello" from outside, followed by the clumping of footsteps coming up the stairs to the main office. Stirling and Olivia exchanged a knowing glance and both said at the same time, "Reynaldo."

"No wonder Lola was barking," said Olivia.

Stirling nodded. "Right. Trying to warn us."

Reynaldo Solis was a loud, vibrant, robust man in his mid-seventies, a real estate magnate and a local celebrity in Progreso. He was also Dr. Stirling's next-door neighbor.

"Hello, everyone," he said with gusto. "Hope I'm not interrupting anything."

"No, you're fine," said Olivia. "Doc just said goodbye to his last patient of the day."

"Where've you been, Reynaldo?" asked Stirling. "It's been a while. How is everything?"

"Very well, thank you. But I wanted to be sure the noise wasn't bothering you."

Olivia and Stirling exchanged puzzled looks.

"What noise?" asked Stirling.

"I'm having some remodeling done." Said Reynaldo. "Adding a new room for Victor. He's moving back in with me temporarily, until he finds someplace else. The damn drills were making Lupita crazy next door. I just wanted to make sure it wasn't bothering you or your patients."

"Haven't really noticed it," Olivia assured Reynaldo.

Stirling's cell phone rang. Glancing at the screen, he saw that it was Irina. He tapped the screen, taking the call. "Hello?"

"Who is it?" Olivia whispered.

Stirling silently mouthed Irina's name. Olivia rolled her eyes. She knew Irina and liked her very much, but nonetheless she still felt some jealousy towards the woman who'd won Stirling's affection, especially since, unlike her, she'd managed to hold onto it.

"I'm here at the office," Stirling said into the phone. "No, in Progreso." There was a pause, and then he said, surprised, "You're kidding...!"

Reynaldo, a natural-born gossip, gave Olivia an inquisitive look and muttered quietly, "Who?"

"His girlfriend," Olivia whispered.

Wishing for some privacy, Stirling stepped away from them and went to the window overlooking the ocean. "It's fine," he said, though he couldn't mask the disappointment. "I just thought we were going to have our weekend together in Cozumel...No, that sounds good..." The tone of his voice brightened. "No, actually, that's perfect. Xcantun. Tonight at 8. Okay, I'll see you then...I love you, too. Bye."

Stirling looked over at Olivia and Reynaldo, both grinning at him.

"Hot date?" asked Olivia.

"Okay, you two," said Stirling, "I have to get going."

"That's okay," said Olivia, beginning to gather her things, Lola at her heels. "Reynaldo and I have very special plans of our own. Right, Reynaldo?"

She batted her eyelids at Reynaldo and he instantly began playing along.

"Oh, yes, my dear. Fine restaurant, moonlight stroll..."

Olivia cooed, "Just you, me, and little Lola..."

With comic opera exaggeration, Reynaldo said, "I love you, Olivia."

In turn, she replied, "I love you, too, Reynaldo."

"Alright, alright," said Stirling, heading for the door. "You have a wonderful evening, Reynaldo. And Olivia…I'll see you on Monday."

"You might," she said, "if I don't run off with Reynaldo." She gave Stirling a wink. And with a smile, he was gone.

Reynaldo held the door open for Olivia as she and Lola exited, and then he stepped out. She pulled her keys from her purse and locked the door, while Reynaldo watched Stirling's BMW pull onto the road and head towards Merida.

"The way he speaks to her on the phone…," said Reynaldo, "It's nice. You can tell he adores her. He seems happy."

Heading down the steps and approaching her own car, Olivia said, with a trace of wistfulness, "Yes. I suppose he does."

9

Hacienda Xcantun was also known as La Casa de Piedra, which literally translated to the House of Stone. A combination restaurant, hotel, and spa, it was known to be one of the more expensive getaways in the whole of Yucatan, a place that prided itself on its world class amenities, exceptional service, and outstanding international cuisine.

Stirling and Irina took their habitual corner table at Hacienda Xcantun and ordered their usual meals—salmon Veracruzana for him, and pollo pibil for her. Having finished their main courses, they now enjoyed the romantic ambiance, a mood enhanced by the intoxicating effects of their second bottle of Merlot.

The general manager, Rolando, swung by their table several times, as was his custom, making sure his loyal customers, Stirling and Irina, were treated like royalty. A sophisticated man in his late forties with an impeccable sense of taste and style, he'd been a friend and confidante of Stirling's for the better part of five years. Coming around again, he asked, "Is everything wonderful this evening?"

"Superb as always," Stirling answered with a smile.

Irina concurred, saying, "You've outdone yourself once again, Rolando. It's the best meal I've had in a long time."

"Thank you, Madam. I am humbled by your presence."

She raised her glass and toasted him.

"Rolando," said Stirling, "would you do us a favor and have them prepare a couple of flans and cappuccinos for us?"

"Whatever El Belizeno Huero wants, El Belizeno Huero gets."

Irina smiled and looked at Stirling curiously, not entirely sure of the backstory behind that particular expression. Stirling shrugged it off.

"I'll have those out shortly," said Rolando as he left them and made his way back to the main dining area.

"Quite a character," said Stirling.

"He's wonderful," agreed Irina. "The place wouldn't function without him."

"You're definitely right about that."

Taking a sip of her wine, she gazed at Stirling dreamily. He was a mercurial man, often difficult to pin down. He had divulged much to Irina over the years, but there were still areas of shadow, hidden layers she had yet to uncover. It kept her in a perpetual state of wonder and mystery, and she loved it. Whenever she tried to pry the secrets loose, she felt him pulling away, becoming even more silent. So she stopped trying. It was enough to know that he was the man for her in every way, shape and form. Let him keep his mysteries, as long as it meant she could keep him. But this one seemed innocuous enough, and perhaps the wine had dulled his defenses, so she asked, "Kent... that name Rolando just called you..."

"What? The man from Belize?"

"That's not what it means."

"No?"

"Of course not. El Belizeno Huero literally means the white one from Belize."

"But I'm not white. I'm a halfer."

"Yes, but you look more white than Latin. Seriously, why did he call you that? He knows you're half-Mexican and half-American."

Stirling felt amused by her inquisitiveness. "Ask him," he said. "He's called me that for as long as I've known him."

Irina sat up a little straighter, fixing him with a raised-eyebrow look. She wasn't letting this one go.

Stirling relented. "Ok..." he said, "you know how my dad was a U.N. diplomat?"

She nodded.

He continued, "Well back in the day, he and my mother traveled and moved around a lot because of his job. No big deal. But when she was about eight months pregnant with me, they were called to Belize for a brief period because of some case my dad needed to intervene in having to do with some politician's diplomatic immunity. It was kind of a disastrous scenario, to put it mildly. So their stay ended up being longer than expected, and as it happened... I was born in Belize City."

Irina nodded. "A Mexican-American born in Belize," she said. "You truly are a man of the world, Kent Stirling."

"No... I'm just a man who happens to be half-American and half-Mexican."

"Who also happens to have born in Belize..."

Stirling shrugged. "Well, it's not as if I planned it that way. I mean, really, I didn't have much say in the matter."

She laughed, disarmed by his humor.

Feeling warm from the wine, he leaned forward and looked at her closely, beginning with the tantalizing hint of her cleavage, then up to the fine shape of her neck, her soft red lips, her almond-shaped brown eyes, her perfectly styled hair…

"Let's get out of here," he whispered.

"Your place?"

He smiled.

It was a moonless night, making the stars in the velvety sky even more vibrant than usual. Kent Stirling's home in Montecristo was also dark, except for a dim light in a second-floor bathroom. It was candlelight, from a single scented candle on the bathroom counter, casting faint illumination over the bodies of Stirling and Irina, in the shower, in the throes of ecstasy.

Their absences from each other stoked the flames of passion so that when they did finally come together, it was an inferno. Stirling's hunger for Irina was insatiable, and he devoured her under the pulsing water of the shower, taking her from behind, her round breasts pressing flat against the steamy glass of the shower door.

He pushed inside her rhythmically until he groaned and shuddered, and she let out a little cry, not of pain, but of intense pleasure, feeling him explode inside her. And then his hands gently swung her around, and cupped her breasts as he suckled her erect nipples.

She tightened her fingers around the hair on the back of his head, and slowly pulled him downward, his lips kissing her breastbone and belly, then licking the hairs of her snatch, shaved into the form of a perfect landing strip, before pressing into her labia and finding her clitoris. All restraint, all borders, all inhibitions were tossed aside, as his unbridled passion sent her into the stratosphere.

The lovemaking continued into the bedroom, where they fell onto the mattress in each other's arms and she climbed atop him, kissed him, rubbed her hands over his lean, hard body, and took him in her mouth, her warm lips gliding from the tip of his shaft to the bottom. And when he was fully engorged, she straddled his hips and locked her eyes on his while she grabbed his cock and pulled it inside her.

They moved together in perfect harmony, pushing and thrusting, twisting and turning, in a sexual fury building to a boil—and then it happened. She came with a hot, intense orgasm, moaning loudly, as Stirling continued to pump, and she shuddered with one climax after another. Then she leaned down and kissed him, and that finished him—he came like a fountain, filling her warm, wet space. She dissolved into his arms.

Exhausted, sweating, laying side-by-side and gazing into each other's eyes, they felt closer than they ever had before. They were both adventurous, uninhibited lovemakers, but tonight was different. There was something new in their coupling, something more than passion. Something more akin to desperation.

"Where did that come from?" she asked.

"I don't know," he said. "But I may as well never make love again, because I don't know if I'll ever, ever top that."

"Maybe not," she sighed. "But think of the fun we'll have trying."

They laughed, and he pulled her closer. "So when are you moving in?" he asked coyly.

"Ready when you are," she said. "But I think we've had this conversation before, and it always ends with you saying you want to wait until you're fully settled in one place…"

Stirling took in a deep breath, and let it out slowly. "As long as I'm dividing my time between the institute here and the hospital in Belize…" He gazed at the ceiling. "We just need more time."

"You mean you need more time," she said, with a note of disappointment. She didn't want to sound clingy or needy, but she did want the security of having the love of her life beside her every night. Looking lovingly into his eyes, she asked, "Soon?"

Stirling pulled her close and kissed her precious lips. "Yes. Soon."

Irina smiled, certain in the knowledge that he meant what he said. And as she settled back in beside him, she noticed the time on the clock—it was almost two a.m. Her smile quickly faded into a slight frown. "I have to leave."

Stirling was puzzled. "At two in the morning?"

"I know, but my aunt and uncle are here from Mexico City, and we're supposed to go tomorrow to visit the ruins of Chichén Itzá." She kissed him and rose from the bed.

"Now who's keeping us apart?"

Stirling watched from his bedroom window as Irina drove away in her blue Lexus, a car as stylish and exotic as the woman driving it. Wearing his silk pajama bottoms, he walked back to the bed and flopped down, hoping to get at least a few hours of sleep before tomorrow morning's scheduled meeting with Star Merida Hospital's Board of Directors.

It was pitch black outside. He tossed. He turned. Tried sleeping on his back, then on his side. But despite all his efforts to relax, he was unable to drift back to sleep, until the digital clock on the night table read four in the morning. And now, finally, he was beginning to succumb…

…and then he heard it.

Mounted on the wall opposite him was an antique clock, a family heirloom from his childhood home in Southern California. The clock hadn't actually worked for years, but he liked the look of it, and the memories associated with it, so he'd put it up in the bedroom. And now it was ticking. A very faint noise—he wondered if he could be imagining it—but the more he focused on it, the louder it became.

Curious, he forced himself up out of bed and stepped over to the clock. He removed it from the wall and examined the wood on the back of it closely.

And in that instant, every window and door in the room locked itself—a horrify series of clicking sounds. It was as if removing the clock from the wall set off an automatic triggering device that sealed shut every opening.

His bedroom had suddenly become a trap.

The old reflexes kicked in. There was no time to waste. He snatched up a chair by the desk and broke the window. Shattered glass flew everywhere. Long shards landed on both the bed and the floor. But there was now a sheet of steel clamped over the window. He had no time to figure out how to circumvent it.

He quickly put on his bedroom slippers to give the soles of his feet protection from the glass shards, then searched frantically around the room for another possible way out. A more pronounced ticking began, seemingly coming from the bed. Stirling looked underneath it and his eyes went wide with shock—he saw a brick of C-4 with a timer attached to it, scheduled with just four more minutes to go.

Again picking up the chair, he tried to pound the door down. It was no use. He suspected there was now a steel sheet on the other side of it, as well. It was as though the trigger from the wall clock reinforced everything with the strength of an iron chamber. He looked about frantically. The clock ticked. Ninety seconds left. Looking up, he saw the trap door in the ceiling that opened to the attic. He'd never really used the attic, and never bothered to get it outfitted with a tele-scoping ladder and pull string to make it easily accessible. He feared it might be sealed shut from the last time the bedroom was painted, but now it was his only hope.

He quickly dragged the desk beneath the attic door. He jumped up on it, but the ceiling was higher than ex-pected, beyond his reach. Hopping down, he again grabbed the chair, got back up on the desk, and hoisting the chair above his head, rammed it against the attic door. It took a couple of tries, but he loosened it and knock it up inside the ceiling.

Now he set the chair atop the desk, stepped up onto the seat, took a deep breath, bent his knees, and launched himself upward. The chair toppled off the desk as his hands just barely grasped onto either side of the opening. With all his strength, he pulled himself up.

He knew there was no time left. His only chance was to run almost the entire length of the attic, smash through the attic window, and drop two stories to the ground.

No time to think. Just act. He bolted for the window as fast as the house slippers would allow. Nearing the win-dow, he put his arms over his face and lunged.

The explosion was massive.

It erupted just as Stirling smashed through the glass, and the concussive force sent him ten feet through the air, toppling into the vacant lot next door. He'd pulled his knees up before he hit the ground, tucking and rolling into weeds high enough to soften his fall.

He lay there for a moment, the wind knocked out of him, struggling to catch his breath and looking up at the black sky made blacker by smoke that rolled and obscured the twinkling stars. Slowly rising to his feet, he looked back to see his home blown to smithereens. Fire rose from both the bedroom and the attic, and now the lower level was catching aflame.

Reeling and groggy, he grabbed his throbbing head, wincing from the pain of both the fall and the blast, his ears ringing violently.

Thank God Irina had left.

Thank God it was only him.

But why him?

There was only one conclusion—he'd been marked. And he knew who was behind it, but he never expected them to return with such savage force.

This was the work of Gavin Weller.

It was the Sandbox.

10

Dawn broke with the flashing lights of Policia Municipal de Merida and Yucatan State Police vehicles cordoning off the area around Stirling's house, where firefighters were still working to put out the blaze, hoses drenching the building.

Stirling stood on the perimeter, watching in a state of silent rage as his once lovely residence continued gradually burning to the ground. The flames were subsiding now, but the damage had been done. What little remained of his home would most likely end up being demolished.

He flagged down one of the local police officers.

"Excuse me?

"Yes, Doctor Stirling?" The policeman, mid-thirties, was clean cut and professional, and felt sympathy for the well-liked doctor whose home had been destroyed.

"May I borrow your phone?" asked Stirling. "I have to make an urgent call."

"Yes, of course," said the policeman, handing Stirling his cell phone.

"Do you mind—I need to call Belize."

"No problem, Dr. Stirling. Just dial the country code before the area code. It's fine."

"Thank you." Stirling dialed the numbers quickly and waited as the phone rang. A familiar voice picked up on the other end—Dr. Diego Tamayo, one of Stirling's senior advisors from the medical center in Belize. Tamayo, an expert surgeon whom Stirling viewed as a mentor, was just awakening when he picked up the phone.

"Diego?...Yes, it's Kent...Sorry to call so early, but unfortunately I've had a...a personal emergency...That's right…I'm afraid I won't be able to make the conference." There was an extended pause as Stirling listened closely and attentively to the man on the other end of the call. Then he continued, "I'll try to have everything sorted out here within the next couple of days but, again…I can't guarantee anything…Yes, I know…I appreciate that…Take care, Diego… Yes… I'll be in touch."

Stirling ended the call and turned to hand the phone back to the young policeman, but couldn't pick him out among the dozens of blue-uniformed men fanning out over the property. He slid the phone into his pocket. The policeman would come back for it soon enough, he assumed. He continued to stand on the sidelines, his body still aching and his mind still reeling from the confusion of the past two hours, some of it spent with a police investigator and doing his best to answer questions without actually giving up any answers.

A man approached from behind and called his name— "Kent!"

Stirling turned and exhaled a sigh of relief. It was his old friend, Sgt. Ariel Manzanero of the Merida Police Department. Their paths first crossed several years ago, when Manzanero's wife, Marisa, was involved in a near-fatal car crash. Stirling performed the operation that saved her life, and since then Manzanero had felt deeply indebted to him.

"Ariel, thank God…," said Stirling.

"Kent…what the hell happened here?" asked Manzanero, surveying the flames still flaring up in the once-palatial home of his good friend.

"I…I don't know," responded Stirling, shaking his head in disbelief.

"I never took you for the type who'd forget to turn off his stove," said Manzanero.

"Ariel, please…"

Manzanero liked to joke to take the edge off serious situations, but he could hear the regret and barely disguised anger in Stirling's voice. His friend was rattled, seeing his home destroyed, and having barely escaped with his life. He was in no mood for jokes.

"Alright, what do you think happened?"

Stirling muttered in a low voice that Manzanero struggled to make out, "How can they be back? How could they have found me?"

"Kent...?"

"Ariel, excuse me..." said Stirling, moving away from Manzanero. He kept walking for a couple of blocks, until he was away from the chaotic scene. He pulled the young policeman's phone from his pocket. He had one more call to make, one he wanted to keep private.

In a home nestled in the corner of a tree-lined street called Mandeville Canyon, located in an exclusive part of West Los Angeles known as Brentwood, Evan Young's cell phone rang. It was 4:30 in the morning. Young had been up past midnight. He was deep into the REM sleep phase, so it took a moment for him to register that the annoying sound he was hearing was his cell phone on the bedside table. It also woke the redhead sleeping beside him. "Are you gonna answer it?" she murmured.

Young's last name was appropriate. At 55, he looked fifteen years younger, with a toned, fit body. He reached for the phone, found it, and looked at the screen through sleep-tired eyes, squinting to make out who was calling. He didn't recognize the number and was tempted to disconnect, but some instinct told him this could be important. He clicked the button, put the phone to his ear, and yawned, "Hello?"

Hearing the voice on the other end, his eyes widened. He was suddenly one-hundred percent awake and alert. "Um...hold on a minute." He pushed back the covers and swung his legs over the side of the bed.

"Who is it?" murmured the redhead.

"Old friend," he said. "Go back to sleep."

He stood up and trudged down the hallway to his office, where he'd have privacy. As he did so, he pressed a seven digit code on the phone's keypad that clicked and reopened the call, sweeping the line for safety.

"Is the line secure?," asked Stirling.

"It is now," replied Evan.

Now in his office, he settled into a padded leather desk chair and rubbed the sleep from his blue eyes. Evan Young was Stirling's former handler. He was also Stirling's one contact from the Sandbox who still lived stateside. Back in the day, they'd run several missions together. As time passed, Young gravitated to the assignments that offered the highest paychecks but whose objectives were not always easy to justify, and their paths diverged. Nevertheless, he was someone Stirling completely and utterly trusted, despite his being a cold-blooded mercenary and ruthless assassin.

"Kent, where the hell have you been for the past five years?"

"In the Yucatan."

"What? How the hell did that happen?"

"I followed my true calling, Evan. I'm a surgeon now, a respected pillar of the community. No more of this fucking agency shit."

Evan closed his eyes and turned his head from the phone momentarily. He could tell by Stirling's tone that he was in very serious trouble.

"Kent...what happened? Why are you calling?"

"I need to know who Weller has on the inside in Latin America who might have had the clout and the contacts to find me."

"Shit, Stirling, the way you fell off the fucking grid, I didn't think anyone would ever find you again. I thought you were home free. God knows, I prayed that you were."

"Evan, I appreciate the concern...but right now I need answers. My house just got blown into the next century and I barely made it out alive."

"And you think it was a professional hit?"

"Classic C-4 detonator rigged to blow everything in sight. Linked to a vintage clock mounted on my bedroom wall. Whoever did it knew exactly what the hell they were doing."

Evan nodded. The last thing he wanted was to get dragged into some shitstorm. But Stirling was a brother-in-arms. You didn't hang your brothers out to dry. It just wasn't done. "Look Kent, I need you to stay where you are. I'm going to make some calls. Follow up with some of my leads. Is this the number where I can reach you?"

"No, but don't worry about it. I'll be in touch with you."

"You got it, buddy. Take care and watch your back."

Evan was about to click off the call when Stirling added, "Evan—it's Weller. He's the only one who could have known where to find me. So watch your back. If he's cleaning house…"

The line went dead. Young lowered the phone, his mind racing. No use going back to bed—he was fully awake now.

Stirling had disconnected when he heard footsteps coming up behind him and turned around to see Ariel Manzanero approaching.

"Fire's almost out," said Manzanero.

Stirling nodded.

Manzanero continued, "You have a place to stay?"

Stirling thought to himself for a moment. He didn't want to put any of his friends in harm's way, but under the circumstances he knew it would be a good idea to lay low for a little while. "I could go to the beach house in Progreso, but I'm not really of a mind to drive out there."

"Don't even think about it. You're staying with us to-night, and for as long as you like."

"I appreciate that," said Stirling, meaning it.

Manzanero managed a half smile and placed his hand on Stirling's shoulder as they walked back down the street to-gether. Stirling had a very slight limp, collateral damage from the explosion and the landing. As they reached the corner and turned, the flashing lights from both the police cars and the fire engines were still silently illuminating the block.

At the opposite end of the street, a sleek black Mercedes pulled up to the barrier where the street had been cordoned off by the cops. The driver parked and got out of the car. It was Ignacio. He slowly moved to the edge of the barrier to take in the scene. He was stunned when he caught sight of Stirling and Manzanero walking towards the latter's car. Stirling climbed into the back seat. Manzanero got into the driver's side, and the car eased silently away from the charred and smoking remains of Stirling's home.

Ignacio tried to take a step forward but an on-site police office at the edge of the street politely placed his hand on his chest to keep him at bay. "I'm sorry sir, but this is a crime scene. I'm afraid you'll have to turn back and find another way through."

Ignacio read the cop's lips completely. He nodded his understanding and gave the officer a slight but polite smile before returning quietly to his car.

He got inside.

The Mercedes drove off as the dark of the night gave way to the pink-blue light of morning.

11

Next door to Montecristo to the east is the colony known as Campestre. Like Montecristo, its residents were among the wealthiest inhabitants of Merida, as evidenced by the opulence of their homes. One splendid example was the house at the corner of 11th and 8th streets, a palatial three-story estate owned by a wealthy family of jewelers. The immaculately-groomed grounds featured amenities such as a tennis court, an Olympic-sized pool, gazebos, and even an outdoor movie theater to entertain guests on hot summer nights.

The challenge of owning such a lavish property was keeping it presentable, and this task fell to a husband and wife duo of domestics, Consuela and Ernesto Echeverria. Consuela was 45-years-old with dark eyes, a slight figure, and dark hair accented with blonde streaks. Ernesto was five years older and a foot taller, standing at over 6 feet. His wiry frame belied an incredible physical strength. Soft-spoken, dependable, and well-mannered, they were highly respected by their employers.

Their duties completed for the week, Consuela and Ernesto left for the weekend. Their car was modest—an older model Toyota Corolla, about what one would domestics drive. Nothing fancy, but it got them where they needed to go. Their employers, a cultured and charming older couple, waved to Consuela and Ernesto as the Corolla backed out of the garage. Their employers insisted they park there because they were embarrassed to have such a vintage beater visible in front of the home, or parked alongside their own Bentley.

Their employers, of course, had done background checks on Consuela and Ernesto before hiring them, and they checked out fine. As they were meant to. Beneath their humble facades, Consuela and Ernesto hid a secret—they were contract killers, merciless assassins who were senior operatives of the Sandbox. Their part-time job as domestics was a cover that allowed them to seem inconspicuously harmless yet gave them access to the secrets of the rich and powerful of Merida.

As Ernesto piloted the car down the tree-lined street, Consuela's cell phone rang. She removed it from the side pocket of her domestic's uniform and answered it. Almost immediately, her tone became officious and condescending.

"What now?" she asked in a frustrated tone. "Oh, for fuck's sake, must we always take care of everything ourselves?" Without even waiting for a response, she ended the call.

"Problem?" asked Ernesto.

"Nothing we can't handle. Stop over at Eladio's before we go home. Seems one of our vendors can't make the cut this month."

"Paco?"

"Who else?"

Ernesto seemed disappointed as he shrugged. He'd hoped for a relaxing and uneventful evening, but that clearly wasn't in the cards. But, business before pleasure. He swung the Toyota Corolla around and headed towards downtown Merida.

Eladio's was a small chain of mid-range restaurants in the Yucatan that offered decent traditional food as well as musical acts. One of the franchises was owned by Ernesto and Consuela, another of their fronts that was useful for laundering payments for unsavory services rendered. The Toyota parked in a small lot beside the restaurant. During lunch hours from 11 a.m. to 3 p.m. and dinner hours from 6 p.m. to midnight, the parking lot was generally full. But the restaurant was closed for the three-hour period between 3 and 6 p.m. It was now 4:20 in the afternoon.

As Consuela and Ernesto entered their establishment, all fell silent. There were eight people inside, men and women in their twenties and thirties who were living on the razor's edge of society, and the wrong side of morality. They were drawn to Consuela and Ernesto by the lure of money and easy access to drugs. And all had hearts of ice, willing to kill for the right price, or if it meant advancement in the organization.

Least among them was Paco Mariscal. A slightly-built man in his twenties, Paco thought he had the world by the balls because he'd had a long lucky streak placing bets at sporting events. But then he fell behind, and as desperation mounted, he became reckless, then downright sloppy. Now he was way behind on the front money Ernesto and Consuela had provided over six months ago; he hadn't paid back a dime. To make matters worse, instead of coming to them and taking ownership of his shortcomings, he'd tried to run and hide. Then he made the mistake of attempting to buy meth from a woman who turned out to be one of Consuela and Ernesto's gang. And now, here he was, seated at a table, afraid and sweating, with a coarse-looking pair of thugs directly behind him.

He looked up as Consuela's voice echoed through the otherwise empty restaurant. "Paco, my love…" She and Ernesto approached him. Consuela forced a smile, but Ernesto looked grim, a dark cloud hanging over him.

Paco's gift was his ability to think and speak quickly. He'd always been able to talk himself out of tough situations, stroking the egos and kissing the asses of his opponents until they gave in, or at least gave him another chance. He believed that, given the opportunity to speak, he could convince anyone of anything; it was his superpower.

"Consuela, Ernie! Just who I was hoping to see." His cheery tone was belied by the nervous sweat trickling down his face.

The rest of the crew looked at their bosses, bemused. This would be fun…

Consuela slithered up to Paco like a cobra preparing to strike, while Ernesto hovered in the background, first cracking his knuckles, then—dangling his arms beside him—flexing his fingers and making fists.

"Paco, Paco, Paco...what are we going to do with you?" cooed Consuela, sitting on the edge of the table in front of him.

Paco blurted out, "Look, I know what you're thinking. If it's about the money, you don't need to worry. You'll get it back. All of it. Why would I cheat someone as beautiful as you, Consuela? Or you, Ernesto. You're like a father to me. I wouldn't cheat my father."

Ernesto rolled his eyes. Was this kid for real?

Consuela rested her foot on the edge of Paco's chair, between his legs. "When?" she asked.

Paco licked his lips. His throat was dry, his heat racing. "Give me two weeks," he said nervously. "You'll have it all with interest."

Consuela casually turned her head to look back at Ernesto, who shook his head from left to right once.

Consuela turned back to Paco, who was shaking like a leaf. "Who are you kidding? Your credit is completely fucked. You owe us six months of back payments. And now you think if you come here and lick my ass and flatter me, we'll forgive all? We were stupid to front your little scheme with the baseball championships."

"And the Leones lost," muttered Ernesto.

Paco's body shook. Tears rolled down his cheeks. "I fucked up. I know. I'm sorry. I'm sorry. But I want to make it right. Okay? Please? Just give me a chance. It's only twenty grand. I only need one lucky break and..."

"Paco!" Consuela cut him off. She hated whiny men.

His hands trembling, Paco wiped his eyes, and muttered, "Haven't I always kept my word? Didn't I always pay you back? Please..."

Consuela leaned forward, putting her hand over the pendant she always wore and delicately fingering it. It was a gold, diamond-encrusted Santa Muerte figure, three inches long. Like a cat toying with a frightened rat, she said in a soothing voice, "Paco, Paco, Paco, my dearest. If you'd come to us sooner, we might have settled this. But you didn't. You thought you could run. You thought you could hide. But we've got you now. And your luck…has run out."

The men to either side of Paco suddenly gripped his arms, holding him fast. One grabbed his hair and yanked his head back. In a flash, Consuela swung her arm out. The men let go of Paco and he flopped to the floor. A thin red line appeared over his throat, and then blood began to gush from it.

Consuela stood and stepped away. Her Santa Muerte pendant was comprised of two pieces. The top part—the figure's head and shoulders—was a sheath that concealed the bottom part, a small handle—Santa Muerte's body—with a one-and-a-half-inch double-edged blade attached. She picked up a napkin from a table, wiped the blade, and slid it back into its sheath. Santa Muerte was a grim reaper, and she'd just claimed her latest soul.

Consuela looked around at the faces of her crew, who appeared unfazed. "Let that be lesson to all of you—no one steals from us." To the two men who had been holding Paco, she said, "Throw that trash in the incinerator."

A cool breeze blew over the warm sands of Progreso Beach, less crowded today than usual, though there were still some locals sailing and jet-skiing. But Sol y Mar was packed; it might have been too breezy for the beach, but people still needed to eat.

Stirling sat at a table in the middle of the restaurant with Olivia. It was their custom to come here for lunch and enjoy a tasty meal before attending to their patients. There were only a couple scheduled for this afternoon, so they had time to unwind.

But Stirling was wound tight. He'd told Olivia about the fire at his house in Montecristo, but he'd been vague about the details. Sitting with him now, she assumed he was still in shock. He'd been unusually quiet and introspective, mostly staring at the surf, watching it roll in and slide back out. He'd hardly touched his Surf & Turf special, while she was almost finished with her blackened salmon salad.

"You're not eating?" she asked.

Jarred from his reverie, he muttered, "Hm? Oh, I'm sorry."

"If I'd known I'd be dining alone today, I might've worn something sexier," she said, as if she didn't look attractive anyway in her green halter top and black mini skirt that showed her shapely legs to advantage, attracting stares from some of the men—and women—in the restaurant.

To placate her, Stirling grabbed the A-1 sauce and doused his steak with it. He carved a hearty piece, but then just stared at it. He wasn't hungry after all.

"You're not good at this," said Olivia.

"Good at what?"

"Hiding the truth."

Stirling sighed. If his suspicions were true, he didn't want Olivia involved. He wanted to keep her and everyone else who was close to him out of harm's way. But perhaps she might be able to help him…"Liv, has anyone been by the office recently? Anyone we don't know?"

She looked at him curiously, not sure what he was getting at. "If you mean patients, we had a couple of referrals walk in last week to make future appointments but that was about it."

"Any strangers? Anyone neither of us are familiar with?"

Olivia thought for a moment. "No. No one comes to mind. It's just been patients and referrals."

"You're sure? No one else?"

She gave him a hard stare. This wasn't like him. "I'm positive."

Stirling nodded, quiet. He wouldn't take it any further than that. If Olivia was certain, he was certain.

"Speaking of patients," she said, "you have Mrs. Solis at 2:30."

"Of course."

He raised his hand to signal the waiter that he was ready for the check. Then he turned his attention back to the boats lined up symmetrically across the azure sea of Progreso. It had taken him a long time to build a new life here, and he'd just about perfected it. The perfect balance between work and relaxation. In the perfect place. With perfect friends. A perfect mate. And now, he couldn't escape the feeling that these pristine days were about to end.

He thought he had outrun his past.

He was wrong.

12

The Power Gym in downtown Merida was one of the trendier, more upscale gyms in the city, with a membership approaching two thousand who kept all three of its levels busy throughout the day. On the ground floor were the weights and cardiovascular section with stationary bikes, treadmills and Stairmasters. The second level featured a kickboxing ring and studios designed for both aerobics and spinning classes. The uppermost level was strictly for executive offices, which were soundproofed and had tinted glass that permitted those inside to look out, but those on the outside couldn't see in.

Outside the gym, a red Range Rover pulled up and parked in a reserved parking space. Inside were Consuela and Ernesto; when they weren't posing as domestics, they lived larger. They emerged from the Range Rover and entered the gym, and though dressed in track suits and sneakers, they swaggered in like they owned the place. Because they did.

Two beefcake employees greeted them as they passed through the front door into the main gym. It was crowded that afternoon. Many of the members recognized Ernesto and Consuela, waving or calling out greetings as the couple strode past them. Reaching the stairs, the duo hustled up to the executive office.

A few minutes later, another person entered, dressed in normal street wear—black tee-shirt, blue jeans and work boots. It was Ignacio. As he passed the front desk, Joaquin—one of two muscle-bound receptionists in too-tight short-sleeved Polo shirts—called out a perfunctory "Can I help you?" It was to no avail—Ignacio kept moving past.

"Sir!," Rocco, the other receptionist, said sternly, "This is a members only club!" Over six-feet tall and carrying two hundred pounds of pure muscle, Rocco stomped over to Ignacio, grabbed his arm just as he was reaching for the door to the gym, and yanked him back, saying, "You got shit in your ears, buddy?"

Ignacio calmly removed his sunglasses, folded the earpieces down, and hung them from the neck of his tee-shirt.

Joaquin came over, standing next to Rocco in front of Ignacio like an impenetrable wall of brawn. Joaquin crossed his arms, Rocco put his hands on his hips. They glared at Ignacio. Joaquin repeated, "Like I said, members only."

Ignacio said nothing.

The two beefcakes exchanged a look. "Must be some kind of retard…" said Rocco.

He wouldn't be saying anything else for a while; Ignacio's stiff, flat hand flew into his windpipe, crushing it. Rocco crumpled to his knees, gasping for air.

Joaquin immediately took a swing at Ignacio, with a mallet-like fist. But he was slow compared to Ignacio, who easily dodged the blow, grabbed the big hand, and shoved it back, snapping the wrist. Joaquin grimaced from the blazing pain. Ignacio spun and smashed the heel of his boot into Joaquin's jaw, dislocating it. Joaquin went down, whimpering in agony.

Ignacio opened the door to the gym and entered. With no one to stop him, he glided across the gym to the stairs and casually trotted up to the executive offices. He opened the door and was taken aback by what he saw—there was a door to his left and another at the end of a long, wide hallway, slightly ajar. The hallway itself was a den of iniquities, dimly lit by a garish red light illuminating a pungent cloud of reefer smoke. The burning-rope smell of the marijuana mixed with a gagging stench of incense, plus there was the odor of sweat and cheap perfume emanating from a woman who looked like a porn star on a sofa straddling a man in a suit, pants around his ankles, riding him like a hobby horse. Just beyond them, a topless brunette with pendulous breasts occupied a couch with two overweight men in expensive suits—local politicians, Ignacio assumed—who were snorting lines of cocaine from the glass table in front of them. At a smaller table next to the far door, two beefy men in Polo shirts, almost carbon copies of Joaquin and Pablo, sat at a smaller table playing poker, with a pile of cash in the pot.

It was like a sea of human vice, and Ignacio blithely sailed through it to the door at the hallway's end. He nudged it open with his shoe and entered cautiously. Seated at a massive wooden desk in front of him was Ernesto, studying a book of accounts, with Consuela looking over his shoulder. Ignacio closed the door behind him and took a couple of steps forward.

Ernesto fixed him with a steely stare and said, "I understand you're the one."

They weren't alone. There were seven other men in the room, some tall, some short, some as muscle-bound as the gym's receptionists, some thin and wiry. Ignacio instantly sensed they were all killers-for-hire. He recognized a few of them. He'd killed the partner of at least one of them.

With a nod from Consuela, all the men rose to their feet and closed in around Ignacio. So that's it, he thought. This was a test. Pass it or die.

Ignacio looked at them curiously, not certain what to make of their appearance.

"You come highly recommended by our friends at the Sandbox," said Consuela.

Ernesto reached underneath his desk and pressed a button. Ignacio didn't hear the door lock behind him, but he didn't have to. He could tell from the thickness of the windows behind Ernesto's desk that the room was sound-proofed. The denizens of the hallway wouldn't hear a thing—and were too drugged-out to care, even if they did.

Ignacio delicately removed his cell phone from his pocket and placed it face down on the desk. Consuela was intrigued and impressed by his cool stoicism. She sat on the corner of the desk, ready to enjoy the show. Ernesto stared coldly into Ignacio's eyes.

Ignacio clenched his fists.

Ernesto leaned back and said, "Gentlemen, fulfill your contracts."

With that command, the attack dogs were unleashed. They formed a circle around Ignacio. He slowly pivoted around, immediately sizing each of them up, waiting for the first one to make a move.

It came from his right. An Asian martial-arts artist opened with a roundhouse kick, aiming for Ignacio's nose. Ignacio ducked and spun, and in an instant had the man's leg and throat in vise-like grips. He flung the man across the room onto a wood and glass coffee table. The glass shattered from the impact, shards flying, along with a polished silver vase of flowers.

One down.

In the reflection of the vase, Ignacio could see two men behind him whipping out switchblades. With near-superhuman speed, he whirled around and clamped his hands around the knife-wielding hand of one of the assailants, then pulled the man forward and plunged the blade into the heart of his partner. The partner fell, aghast, blood pouring into the carpet. Ignacio let go of the other's hand and snapped his elbow up with enough force to crack the thin layer of bone in his temple. The man crumpled.

Three down. One dead, two reeling.

Ernesto and Consuela watched with bated breath. A wave rippled through Consuela's voluptuous body; she was turned on by the bloody battle.

Now came the fourth man, swinging a chain above his head like a lasso. Ignacio focused his attention on the big man's eyes. He knew the secret to hand-to-hand combat was to stay focused on your opponent's eyes, not his weapon.

The man swung the chain at Ignacio's head. Ignacio rolled forward, leapt up, and jammed the switchblade—which he grabbed from his dying previous foe in mid-roll—into the new opponent's eye. The big man stumbled backwards, hands going to his blinded eye, dropping the chain—which Ignacio now caught.

Four down. Two dead.

His first opponent had now extricated himself from the shattered coffee table and rushed forward, grasping a pointed shard of glass. He slashed at Ignacio, swiping across his chest, ripping open his shirt and leaving Ignacio with a thin red scratch. Before he could lunge again, Ignacio wrapped the chain around his neck and yanked back. There was a loud snap.

Four down. Three dead.

Ignacio was getting tired. He needed to end this quickly, so instead of waiting for the fifth attacker to lunge, he charged into the man like a locomotive. He jumped up into a forward flip and knocked the man off balance, smashing him to the ground. Ignacio quickly jabbed his knee firmly into the man's back while simultaneously grabbing his jaw with both hands and yanking upward. The man's spinal cord broke with a chilling snap that sent a rush of arousal coursing through Consuela.

Five down. Four dead.

The sixth man was built like a brick wall, wide and stout with mitts like iron mallets. He raised them and assumed a boxer's stance. So he wanted to spar...okay. Ignacio would oblige.

They began circling each other, fists up. The man swung a left jab, catching Ignacio's chin. No blood drawn, but the pain put Ignacio on alert. He sidestepped another punch and countered with a striking straight hand to the man's throat, fingers pointed forward, crushing the man's Adam's apple in the process. He followed with a flurry of side-kicks that pummeled the thug's mid-section and his face. The man was dazed, barely standing, wheezing for breath. A finishing blow was all that was needed. Ignacio dealt a powerful roundhouse kick that broke the manis neck. He fell forward with a resounding thud that shook the room.

Six down. Five dead.

The final man stood in front of Ernesto's desk, protecting his employer. He was about Ignacio's size and wore dark sunglasses.

Ignacio energy was waning. This final henchman would have to go quickly. In one last balletic movement, Ignacio gracefully leapt forward and slid across the floor on his knees towards the seventh man.

The man's hand grabbed each side of his belt buckle and yanked, and he was now holding two short blades. But before he could put them to use, Ignacio struck a hard fist to the man's solar plexus. He then snatched the blades out of the man's loose grips and plunged them deep into the jugular veins on each side of his neck. The man's eyes rolled upward as his blood fountained out of the wounds. He collapsed to the carpet, bleeding out. Some of his blood splashed onto Consuela's face. She wiped it away, titillated.

All down. One left alive. And his skull was cracked, his breathing erratic. Ignacio calmly picked up a shard of glass, knelt beside the man, and sliced his throat.

Seven down.

Seven dead.

Someone had a hell of a mess to clean up, thought Ignacio, himself spattered with blood, none of it his own save for the minor cut across his chest. He looked at Consuela, who was aroused by the deadly combat. Her eyes scanned

Ignacio from head to foot and back up again. With a satisfied smile, she cooed, "So it is him."

Ernesto leaned forward. "Tell me, what can we do for you…Viper?"

Ignacio reached for the cell phone he had placed on Ernesto's desk. Lifted it up, pressed a few buttons, swiped, and held the face of the phone in front of Ernesto's eyes, showing the crime boss a full-length photograph, taken from a distance, of Dr. Kent Stirling.

13

Inside the Stun Modeling Agency on the Paseo Montejo in Merida, Heidi Aronson spent the morning reviewing new modeling candidates, all of whom had aspirations to be the next Heidi Aronson. In her day, Heidi was in great demand, traveling the world on assignments, gracing the covers of magazines from Rio to Paris to New York City, dating actors and rock stars and politicians. It was a grand adventure while it lasted, but it couldn't last forever. Good lighting and professionally applied make-up could hide many imperfections, but they couldn't keep a model looking 20-years-old forever.

However, even in her mid-thirties, she was a striking woman, and intelligent to have invested her earnings, and her name recognition, into a business she knew inside and out. She began her own modeling agency and within a few short years had a highly sought-after stable of young women. She taught them the tricks to succeed and the pitfalls to avoid, gave them the benefit of her knowledge and took from them enough of a commission to support herself in a relatively grand style.

Today's candidates were a mixed bag. Some were beautiful in the conventional sense, some striking in a way that could be off-putting, but from the right angle, were captivating. Some were too thin, some too heavy, some too taken with themselves, some not taken enough. It took a particular mix to be a supermodel, to withstand the rigors of the assignments, the egos of the people at the height of the profession, and avoid the temptations that presented themselves with boring regularity. Too many of the friends she made on the way up succumbed to those temptations and ended their careers prematurely. If nothing else, she'd spare her proteges that fate.

At mid-day, she exited the agency and couldn't help but notice a well-dressed man standing at the front of a Mercedes, its hood up, hunched over the engine. There was something familiar in his posture, his broad shoulders, the hair pulled back in the small ponytail…and then she remembered. It was the man she'd encountered at Sol y Mar.

She crossed the street to him, but instead of coming up behind, she arced around to approach him from the side, so he could see her and not be startled. And see her he did. In her beige min-dress, bare, tanned legs, and hair brushed back but for a lock dangling over her right eye, she couldn't be missed. When his eyes met hers, he smiled in recognition. She signed to him, "What are you doing here?"

Ignacio rose to his full height and signed, with grease-stained fingers, "Car stalled. Can't get the engine to turn over. I figured I'd see if I could get it started myself. Might be the alternator."

She responded, "Let me have a look."

"You know cars?"

"I know a lot of things."

He gave her a bemused look, but stood back. She came around to the side of the car, tugged at spark plug cables, checked the wiring around the alternator, and looked for any loose connections or signs of fuel leakage, but couldn't see anything obviously wrong. Then, on a hunch, she walked to the driver's side and opened the door.

"What are you doing?" he signed.

"Just going to try to start it," she replied. And as soon as she opened the door, climbed in, and glanced at the floorboard, her suspicions were confirmed. She got back out and stepped over to Ignacio.

"Where is it?" she asked him, with an accusatory smile.

He shrugged innocently.

She continued, "You shouldn't have left the fuse box cover off. Where's the ignition fuse?"

She had his number. He grinned sheepishly, wiped his hand on a rag and, reaching into his pocket, pulled out the fuse.

"If you wanted to see me," she signed, "you could have just rang the bell. You obviously knew where to find my agency. Why not announce yourself? Or are you really that shy?"

She really had his number. "Cautious," he replied.

"Where are you staying?" she asked.

Ignacio was reluctant to respond. He was in unfamiliar territory now. For almost every second of every day of his adult life, he'd been totally in control. But not this second. She'd turned the tables on him. She was running the show now. And he had to decide if he'd take the chance or not. He felt an emotion he'd never experienced before—longing.

He took the leap, signing, "In Progreso."

"Where in Progreso?"

"The Tropical Suites."

"Good," she signed, with a gleam in her eyes. "Now I know where to find you."

She pointed to emphasize "you," then spun around and continued on her way.

Ignacio watched her go, knowing they would see each other again, and soon.

Los Pinos was a community where both the middle-class and upper middle-class of Merida resided. It was not as exclusive as Montecristo, but was just as safe, owing to the number of higher-ranking law enforcement members who lived there, including Ariel Manzanero.

Manzanero's home was designed in a Greco-Roman style, with a teal-colored exterior and spiral outdoor staircase. In back of the house was a large black-bottom pool; in front was a rose garden as colorful and ordered as one might expect in a city park. The home was a step above the others in the area, owing to Ariel having been so involved in its construction. He'd spent two years supervising it, and moved in after he and Marisa were married. Now, it was the home in which they were raising their two young daughters, Mireya and Lysette.

Tonight, it was also hosting Dr. Kent Stirling, whose BMW was parked in front. He'd brought Irina with him for dinner and now, having eaten, the adults had retired to the cool fresh air of the patio to enjoy flan and homemade coffee.

"Delicious," Stirling said to Marisa.

"Yes," agreed Irina. "It's wonderful. You've outdone yourself, again."

Ariel gave Marisa a loving look. He adored his wife, and felt tremendous gratitude to Stirling for having saved her life all those years ago.

Marisa, ever the proud mother, deflected the compliment from herself by saying, "You know, I forgot to mention that Mireya won the tennis tournament for her age group at the Country Club."

"It's true," said Ariel proudly. "We may have a future pro on our hands. She's taking it very seriously. Thinks it will win her a scholarship to college."

"Don't hold her back," said Stirling. "Maybe one day her passion will become her profession. We all have a destiny in this life, Ariel."

"Absolutely," agreed Irina. "Here's to Mireya...the next Serena Williams."

Marisa nodded proudly, as Ariel took her hand in his and gave it a squeeze.

The moment was interrupted by the ringing of Ariel's cell phone.

"No phones at the table, Ariel," said Marisa. "You know that."

Ariel glanced at the phone. "Sorry, darling. I'm been expecting this." He stood, looking at Stirling and Irina. "Excuse me, please."

He went inside and headed for his study. As he clicked to answer the call, Stirling noticed he was speaking in a clipped but hushed tone, as though he didn't want his guests to overhear. He went into the study and closed the door.

Irina took it in stride but Stirling had an inkling the call might be about him. His focus drifted from the ladies' conversation to what might be transpiring behind the study door.

Marisa, who'd been eyeing Irina's pendant all evening, took this opportunity to ask about it. Hanging from a gold herringbone chain, it showed a leaping panther cast in 24-carat gold.

"That's a stunning piece, Irina. Where did you get it?"

Irina touched her fingers to it. "Oh, this? Stirling gave it to me."

Impressed, Marisa asked him, "Kent, where did you find such a lovely piece?"

Stirling wasn't listening. Irina noticed, and said, "Kent?"

He snapped out of it, and looked at the women. "I'm sorry, what?"

"Marisa asked you a question."

Stirling gave Marisa an inquisitive look. She said, "I was just wondering where you found that beautiful pendant Irina is wearing."

"Oh, it was a gift. Second year anniversary. Had it made specially for her at one of those old-school jewelers downtown."

"Why a panther?"

Stirling glanced at Irina. She smiled coyly and chuckled, "Stirling thinks I may have been a panther in my previous life."

Marisa raised a wicked eyebrow. "Really? I wonder why..."

The women laughed. But Kent's attention was again focused on the study door.

"Kent?" queried Irina. His eyes snapped back to her. "Are you alright?"

"Fine," he said. "I just need to excuse myself. All that coffee."

Marisa said, "You know where to find it."

Stirling rose from the table and headed inside and down the hallway, in the direction of the restroom—and the study.

When the women were alone, Marisa asked Irina, with concern, "Is he alright?"

"About as well as can be expected," she answered.

"So terrible, to lose all you have in a flash. And all because of a gas leak."

Stirling paused outside the study, his ear close to the door. He could only make out bits of Ariel's conversation inside: "Just keep a close eye on them...Don't let them out of your sight. If the trail goes cold, alert our people in Campeche...Exactly...Update me once the contact arrives."

He knew Ariel had signed off the call. Hearing his friend approaching the door, Stirling quickly and quietly took a few steps back, to the bathroom. He ducked in, flushed the toilet, and reemerged to see Ariel coming towards him, having left his study. "Everything alright?" Stirling asked.

Ariel said quietly, "That was a lead regarding your case."

"What have you found out?"

Ariel looked out at the women, who were immersed in their own conversation. He continued, "We had a tip from someone who works at the Power Gym. They said a deal's going down at the Luna Azul Saturday night involving the local syndicate and some mystery man from out of town."

"Nothing unusual about a dope deal going down."

"I didn't say it was a dope deal."

Stirling, intrigued, "What is it, then?"

"Unclear. But I've ordered one of our detectives to tail our contact at the gym."

"Who's the contact?"

"Used to be one of our street snitches. But then he moved up in the world. Went to work for the head of the syndicate."

Stirling nodded. "Appreciate the information, Ariel. You'll keep me informed?"

Ariel nodded. "Of course, Kent. You know I've got your back."

Stirling knew Ariel meant what he said. But he also knew there was little his friend could do to protect his back if, indeed, the Sandbox had painted a target on it.

14

Ignacio leaned against the rail of his third-floor room's balcony, clad only in tight-fitting blue jeans. He stared out at the ocean as the sun descended, beginning its metamorphosis from blinding white light to bright red ball the closer it came to the horizon line. When he was a child, he was told that if he watched until it disappeared into the ocean, he'd see a green flash. Sometimes he did. It wasn't magic, just biology—staring at the red orb for so long caused the eye to retain an afterimage in its complementary color, green, for a few seconds once it was gone. Just an illusion.

The Tropical Suites, being the only hotel on Progreso's main drag that directly faced the Gulf of Mexico, caught a direct cool breeze wafting in off the water. The breeze made Progreso less humid than Merida, and the temperature at night was perfect. The beach area wasn't as lively as Merida after dark, and the amenities of the Tropical Suites not as plentiful and up-to-date as the more cosmopolitan city's luxury hotels, but the austerity of the establishment suited Ignacio.

He sat in a wicker chair on the balcony, continuing to watch the sunset, introspective, worrying that he might be losing his edge. Kent Stirling should already be dead. He should already have collected his bounty from the Sandbox. But this doctor had proven to be more resourceful than most. And now the Viper had enlisted help—Ernesto and Consuela. And they'd had the temerity to make him prove himself. In retrospect, he wondered if he might not have been better off killing Ernesto and Consuela rather than the seven assassins they arrayed against him. Their testing of him wasted a lot of good talent. A couple of them he'd crossed paths with before. He never would again.

This whole mission seemed to be tilting sideways, and he wasn't helping things by his clumsy pursuit of Heidi. He was impressed that she'd seen through his broken-down car ruse so quickly. She had an exceptional mind to complement her extraordinary good looks. And she was right—he should have just gone into her office and approached her, instead of playing games like a lovesick teenager. But what was the point, anyway? He'd be gone soon, off to another assignment.

There was no future in relationships for Ignacio. There never was. At best, he could indulge in a one-night stand, or a brief fling. He wasn't above sleeping with another man's wife to extract information; married women often felt protective of Ignacio because of his handicap, and most felt some neglect from their husbands, so they poured their secrets out to him. It didn't matter that he was mute. They appreciated that he let them do all the talking. And he was such an attentive listener.

To escape his thoughts, he went back inside and decided to distract himself by doing something routine. He pulled one of the large cases out from under the bed and placed it atop the bedcovers. Snapping the latches, he opened the case. Inside, snugly fit into pockets cut to their specific shapes in soft foam, were the components of a long-range sniper rifle. Sitting where he could face the door to his room, his back to the open sliding glass door of the balcony, Ignacio took the pieces out one-by-one and carefully and delicately cleaned them.

This was Ignacio's tool of choice for removing targets. He'd used it many times before, in locations such as Rome, Paris, London, New York, and Mexico City, each time retiring a mark given to him by the Sandbox or some other organization willing to meet his price. He'd even played both sides of the fence, having been hired for one assignment by the Soviets, and for another by the Americans. He didn't care about politics. He cared about the job, about how challenging it would be and how much it paid.

Oiling and wiping the barrel, he suddenly froze.

He'd noticed a movement out of the corner of his eye. He looked to the door. There was a shadow beneath the door jamb. Someone standing on the other side. He quickly shoved the rifle components under the bed, not bothering to put them back in the case, which he shoved in after them.

In a flash, he was at the door. He carefully leaned forward to peer through the peephole. And he was stunned. Standing outside his door, holding a bulging bag of groceries, was Heidi—the one person he'd hoped to see, and yet hoped not to see. But the sight of her in her form-fitting aqua-colored top, short black skirt, and knee-high black boots overcame his defenses.

He would take the risk.

He unlocked and opened the door.

As soon as she saw him, Heidi's face broke into a smile. Her eyes lit up. And so did Ignacio's. He stepped back, holding the door open, and she entered. She carried the grocery bag to the kitchen counter, set it down, and signed, "I hope you haven't had dinner."

"No," he replied, watching in delighted amusement as she unpacked the bag—a bottle of wine, vegetables, a baguette, a couple of slabs of fish.

Ignacio signed, "You don't have to go to any trouble. We could go out to dinner, if you'd like."

Her eyes took him in, from his too-tight jeans to his lean, toned body to that handsome face and those icy blue eyes that, rather than being a mirror to his soul, were a barrier; that's what intrigued her. She replied, "Do you really think I would have brought my favorite wine over if I wanted you to take me to dinner?"

He was intrigued with her, also. He asked, "How did you find me?"

"I have friends in high places," she responded, "and also among certain car dealerships."

Ignacio grinned. He had to admire her—part fashion model, part Sherlock Holmes. And also, apparently, part chef—she was already scouring the drawers for cooking utensils.

"Do you like your Mahi Mahi grilled or blackened?"

"Black," he signed, "like my heart." He smiled. She guffawed.

He assisted her with the food preparation, beginning with slicing the vegetables. He really knew his way around a knife, she thought…and then she noticed the bruises on his arms and back, some yellow, some deep blue, and the slight scar across his stomach. With a look of concern, she asked, "What happened?" She pointed at his scars.

He shrugged. "Some guys tried to mug me," he signed. After a pause, he added, "They didn't succeed."

Wow, she thought, this man's a badass. Some women would run from a man like that, but Heidi was no shrinking violet. She liked a little danger in her men.

While the fish was cooking, he escorted her out to the balcony, where they sipped wine and watched the sunset. She looked even more beautiful in the soft evening light. His instincts told him to push her away, don't get involved, don't let down his guard, don't let her in. His heart told him to kiss her.

He listened to his heart.

He lowered his head to give her a gentle kiss, which she accepted, and returned, her hand snaking around his bare back. They held the kiss, each one feeling an electric impulse course through them. And when their lips parted, she took a step back, looked at him seductively, and signed, "I'm hungry. You?"

"Famished," he replied.

Neither one was talking about dinner.

Ignacio turned off the stove, and they turned up the heat.

She stepped beside his bed, sat on the edge, and pulled off her boots. Then she stood and unbuttoned her blouse, dropping it to the floor. Next she unzipped her black skirt and let it fall. Now only in a black lace bra and panties, she padded around to the other side of the bed, allowing Ignacio to take in the sensuous curves of her body. She unsnapped her bra, and slowly pulled it free from her breasts, smiling, teasing him, satisfied at the growing bulge in the crotch of his jeans. Her breasts were luscious, the nipples erect in the cool breeze coming through the open sliding door of the balcony. Continuing to tease him, she slid beneath the sheets, her eyes still locked on his, pulled her knees up, and removed her panties. She dropped them over the side of the bed.

Now it was his turn. He stepped slowly to the side of the bed, taking his time unbuttoning and unzipping his jeans, then pulled them down below his knees and stepped out of them. He stood naked in front of her, erect, pulled back the covers, and took a long look at her body, her round breasts, her soft tummy, her shapely legs, velvety thighs, and the tantalizing tuft between them.

Ignacio's lovemaking was not what she expected; she imagined he might be rough, take her quickly, and then ease off to sleep, as so many of the rich and powerful men—and some women—she'd slept with had done. But he was different. He was tender. His fingers glided over her breasts barely touching them, circling her nipples, and then he kissed them, his tongue dancing over them. Then he kissed her neck, her cheek, and—pausing to look deeply into her eyes—her lips. A long, languorous kiss. And his hand, ever gentle, barely touching her, glided downward. And his long, delicate fingers sent her into ecstasy.

She totally gave herself over to him, and he took his time, as though this might be the last time he'd ever have such an experience, and he was determined to make it memorable. His teasing foreplay seemed to go on for hours, his versatile tongue finding the most sensitive of her erogenous zones and sending her into an orgasm that left her writhing and wet. And then he entered her, slowly, keeping his eyes locked on hers, looking, it seemed, into her very soul.

He began to gently thrust, and she did, too, timing her hips to be in perfect rhythm with his, an erotic dance that they extended for as long as possible, until he knew he was about to erupt, and then he reached down and, while he continued entering her, pressed his fingertips on her clitoris and massaged. Her body suddenly quaked with a shivering orgasm, at the same moment he came inside her.

When it was over, she rolled onto her side, catching her breath. And he lay on his side, one hand propping up his head, the other gently massaging her back. Her eyes were misty. She'd never experienced anything like this. She'd shagged, she'd fucked, she'd had her fun, but she'd never truly made love…until now. And then she realized that, unlike so many of the men she'd been with, Ignacio wasn't just screwing her for his own satisfaction; he was more concerned with hers. And making it as fabulous as it could be for her gave him pleasure.

She rolled onto her back, looking up at his handsome face. He gently wiped a tear from the corner of her eye. And in that moment, he knew he'd crossed a line that he vowed he would never cross. There was no turning back. He'd committed a transgression that would put both his life and hers in incalculable danger.

He'd fallen in love.

15

About twenty-seven miles southwest of Merida sat Uman, a smaller town that was primarily an industrial center for self-made men whose companies were affiliated with larger corporate industries. But despite its modest appearance, Uman had an old and rich history; the archeological sites at the villages of Bolon, Hotzus, and Kizil were all adjacent to the center of Uman, and the Hacienda Yaxopoil, also known as "the Place of the Green Alamo Trees," was a popular tourist attraction.

With a population of only a few thousand, Uman was a small enough place that everyone seemed to know one another. Yet very few had heard of a local electronics wizard and small time inventor named Bernie Llewelyn. In his late sixties with a distinguished aura of life experience and piercing blue eyes, Bernie was an American expat of Scots-Irish extraction who had been living in a state of near-anonymity in Uman for several years, which was just how he liked it.

Near a local eatery called Ruben y Lalo, Bernie had a small electronics repair shop with a tiny, innocuous sign in front that said, "TV REPAIR." His Spanish was not fluent but it was serviceable—he could communicate well enough—and the locals knew and respected Bernie.

His next-door neighbor was a grandmother, Elda Lara, and her three grandchildren, aged 22, 14 and 10, were all boys. They had lost their parents several years ago, when they were mugged in Merida by lowlifes who shot and killed them. But Elda Lara had done a magnificent job of parenting her grandchildren; now, the eldest son, Humberto, was one of the assistant managers at the local bank. The younger boys, when not busy with their schooling, helped Elda Lara with a small restaurant she owned on the border of Merida and Uman that catered to both locals and tourists. And on occasion, Bernie dropped in for a traditional Yucatecan dinner of Pozole and Cochinita Pibil.

In the evenings, Elda Lara liked to watch television, and had been using the same one since before the boys were born. But now the TV was on the fritz, so Humberto brought it into Bernie's shop. It was heavy, even though the screen was no bigger than a 10-inch diagonal. Bernie recognized the model as soon as Humberto stepped inside.

"I haven't seen one like that in years," he said.

"I'll bet," chuckled Humberto. "Think you can fix it? The screen just went black last night in the middle of Grandma's telenovela."

Bernie had a pretty good idea what was wrong even before he'd loosened the screws to the plastic casing. His suspicions were confirmed—one of the old-fashioned tubes inside was burned out.

"You know, your grandmother might want to consider a new set. I hear there's this pretty neat invention now called color TV."

Humberto laughed. "I hear you, Bernie. But she's sentimental about this TV. I think she's had it for, like, forty years. It was a gift from my Grandpa."

"I understand," Bernie nodded. He looked into a "junk box" on a shelf behind him, filled with all sorts of odd nick nacks, including an assortment of ancient vacuum tubes. "Yeah, I can fix it." He shoved the box back onto the shelf. "How's work treating you?"

"Great! I'm training to be a manager. Hopefully I'll have the position by the end of next month."

"Little young to be a manager, aren't you? That's a big responsibility. Sure you can handle it?"

"You know me, Bernie. I had to start young to help grandma makes end meet. But hey, I'm a fast learner. I'm looking forward to it."

Bernie knew Humberto was a bright young man; he'd do just fine. "Well, good luck to you, kid. Come by tomorrow night. I'll have it good as new."

"Thank you, Bernie." After a bit more small talk, Humberto headed out of the shop.

Bernie glanced at his watch. It was almost 9 p.m. Time to close shop. He rolled down the metal warehouse door, and secured it with a chain and padlock. And now, left alone, he could drop the façade and be his true self—the Bernard Llewelyn who'd formerly been with NATO intelligence, an expert in high-tech surveillance and mechanical spy devices, until he became an instructor at the Sandbox. Now here he was, living like a hermit in a Yucatan village. Like Consuela and Ernesto, his humble trappings were a cover that allowed him to hide in plain sight.

Alone now, he picked up Elda Lara's television, ambled to the back of his shop, and opened a door to a closet. Inside, an array of tools were tossed haphazardly. He stepped into the closet and shut the door. Standing in the middle of the floor, he opened a small hidden panel in the wall and pressed a button. The floor began to descend. The closet was actually an elevator.

When it came to rest, Bernie opened the door and stepped out into his underground living quarters and workshop. Unlike the modesty of the shop above, here there was a sizable apartment that included a bedroom with a flat screen TV, overflowing bookcases, and a queen-sized bed, as well as a bathroom with shower/bathtub combo, clothes closets, and a kitchen area with all the amenities one might need to comfortably last out a nuclear holocaust.

A few brick pillars and an archway separated the living quarters from the workshop, on the wall of which were mounted a few vintage firearms, a nickel-plated .45 caliber pistol, a Mac-10 machine pistol, and a sawed-off riot shotgun. Bernie was, if nothing else, a cautious man, and one with a colorful past. He'd seen men die in front of his eyes, including good friends and vile enemies, and had even been the instigator of some of those early retirements. He had no family, no loved ones, no current lovers, nothing to tie him down. He could, if necessary, go elsewhere and disappear at a moment's notice. He knew there were people in the world who would love to see him pay, dearly, for his past transgressions, and thus he lived in relative obscurity, literally underground.

It was far too quiet that evening as he tinkered with the television set. Bernie picked up a small remote control from the table and pointed it over his shoulder. He pressed a button. Within seconds, the entrancing strains of Ravel's Bolero began to reverberate throughout the room. That was better. It gave Bernie the sense of calmness he needed to work in peace, and contemplate a long-held ambition. Like so many others in his line, he'd been burned by the Sandbox. And he would settle the score.

Josh Alan was the product of a union between a prominent New York real estate lawyer and a veterinarian with a thriving practice. They were already in their 40s when they had Josh, who was their only child. He was never very ambitious, but was bright enough to earn an engineering degree from Clark University in Worcester, Massachusetts. Upon graduation, he took a Caribbean vacation with some friends from college, and the excursion forever changed his life. He fell in love with the sea, and found his engineering skills useful for the maintenance of boats. He never looked back. At heart, he was a beach bum who managed to stay employed tending to the yachts of wealthy, well-connected people who admired his skill as a boat captain and genuinely enjoyed his warm, outgoing manner.

His parents had both passed away a few years ago, first his father, then just a couple of months later, his mother, who'd seemed lost without her lifelong companion. And when their estate was settled, Josh Alan inherited a veritable fortune. He bought a yacht of his own and began traveling extensively around the globe, exploring the oceans and visiting some of the most magical places on the planet.

But of all the places where he'd momentarily set anchor, his favorite was Progreso Beach in the Yucatan. For the first time in his life, he put down roots, of a sort, opening a small jet ski and parasailing business. The business did quite well, with the constant influx of tourist almost year-round. Though he'd never have to work another day in his life, he liked having work to give structure to his days, and he genuinely enjoyed his clientele and being of service to the locals and vacationing visitors.

Now well into his forties, he was still quite fit and tan and had a youthful, boyish persona. Women of all ages and from all backgrounds found this attractive, so he very seldom spent a night alone. He was regarded as a Casanova, a reputation he felt obligated to maintain.

After the first year, he hired a rotating crew of young locals to run his shop, so he could spend more time on his true love—restoring and maintaining the sailboats and yachts of his close friends. Friends like Dr. Kent Stirling.

Stirling owned an imposing, impressive-looking yacht called the Lady of the Seas. Stirling's pride and joy, she was 260 feet in length and had seen some rough voyages in the past. Now Josh was giving her a stem-to-stern restoration, inside and out. He had her almost fully restored, and Stirling was rightfully impressed by his friend's tasteful sense of design and craftsmanship.

As Josh painted the upper deck a walnut-brown varnish, lending the vessel a classy, European degree of elegance, Kent approached, ambling down the dock, a cold, sweating bottle of beer in each hand. They'd been friends for half a dozen years, ever since meeting over a casual game of volleyball at a mutual friend's weekend getaway, when they quickly discovered they shared a common interest in sailing and the sea. "Josh," called Stirling, "I've said it before, and I'll say it again—you really missed your calling."

"Just a pastime," said Josh. "Used to help my dad do all the handyman things around the house. Never meant to make a profession of it."

"Admit it—you love it."

"Well, not a bad way for an old beach bum to spend the day."

"A very privileged beach bum."

"Says the very privileged doctor."

"Let me ask you something—if you had to choose between being a poor beach bum, or a wealthy anything else, which…"

"Beach bum," Josh blurted out, before Stirling finished his sentence. "All day, every day. I'd rather be happy than rich. Just dumb luck I ended up being both." He wiped his brush on the side of the pail, then laid it flat on top. Standing up, he wiped his hands on his shorts and crossed over from the boat to the dock.

Kent handed one of the cold beers to him. "Good to know what you want," he said.

"That it is," said Josh. The icy beer took the edge off the hot, humid day. "What about you?" he asked Stirling. "You always want to be a doctor?"

Stirling didn't answer immediately. The events of the past few days had made him more introspective than usual, more prone to pause and think before responding. But after a moment, he said, "In fact, I did. It's one of the two things in my life that I am absolutely certain of. That and…" He hesitated. The other thing he was sure of was that, after the destruction of his home in Montecristo, he was lucky to be alive, and each moment he breathed might be his last.

"And… what?" asked Josh.

Stirling snapped back into the present moment and deflected the conversation away from what he was really thinking. "And Irina," he said. "How much I adore Irina."

Josh nodded. "Yeah. I get that. Though honestly, I don't know what she sees in you. A handsome man, living in paradise, independently wealthy, with a great career, doing service to the community…and, I might add, a yacht that will soon be the envy of the Yucatan, when I'm finished with it."

Stirling smiled. "I guess we both have much to be grateful for."

Stirling remained at the dock long enough for Josh to take him aboard the Lady of the Seas and show him how the renovation was progressing. Josh assured him the yacht would be ready in a week's time—maybe sooner, if the weather cooperated.

Stirling would like to have stayed and pitched in, but he had other, more important work that afternoon. He was due to perform a heart surgery for Santiago Guerrero, a 58-year-old man who'd been a lifelong drinker and smoker. As the years passed, those vices took a toll on his heart. What began as shortness of breath and minor palpitations worsened over the years until he was diagnosed with severe blockages in all four major arteries of his heart. An architect and family man, and an inherently decent person, he'd been a patient of Stirling's for a few years, since being referred by his general practitioner. And now he was a walking time bomb, prone to a fatal heart attack at any minute. He'd already endured two minor ones, but despite that, he was adamantly opposed to the surgery, fearful of being sliced open, even by so skillful a surgeon as Stirling. But Stirling informed him very plainly that if he didn't take the risk, he'd never live to see his grandchildren grow.

So, today he was receiving a quadruple bypass, with Stirling the head surgeon in charge of the operation, assisted by a hand-picked staff of more-than-capable doctors and nurses. They were quiet in the operating room, not wanting to distract Stirling with casual conversation, even if the procedure was relatively routine. Stirling knew that a man's life was literally in his hands, and he'd promised Guerrero's wife, who'd said to him in the waiting room beforehand, "Please save my husband," that he would do just that. Yet, after the events of recent days, he found it difficult to stay focused, to keep the images of his burning house, and the certainty that he'd been targeted, from intruding into the forefront of his mind.

Ten hours in, they were nearing the end. Guerrero's vitals were responding strongly. There was severe blockage near the upper aorta which had hardened and required more time and more finesse than usual, but once they were past that hurdle, the left common carotid artery was fine and functioning, as was the left subclavian artery.

The surgery was a success, but it left Stirling exhausted. But he'd earned the privilege of indulging in his favorite part of surgery—being able to tell the patient's spouse that their loved one was out of the woods and would be recovering shortly.

He found Mrs. Guerrero in the waiting area. A short, slight woman, she hadn't really slept in the past two days and it showed; the stress of hanging on between hope and despair had taken its toll. As Stirling approached her slowly, she rose and staggered toward him with bated breath. When she saw him smile, she burst into tears of relief and joy. She fell into Stirling's arms and held him tightly, bawling into his chest. His powerful arms caressed her and held her until she was able to compose herself. Her gratitude touched him; his own eyes misted. He blinked the tears away and reassured her that all would be well, now. She replied with a chant of gratitude repeated over and over:

"Thank you, Doctor…Thank you…Thank you…"

The following afternoon found Stirling on Merida's Paseo Montejo, which was teeming with people enjoying the pristine weather. Outside the popular Impala restaurant, Stirling sat on a bench beneath a large oak tree reading the newspaper. He was dressed casually in civilian clothes—khaki slacks and short-sleeved shirt, his eyes masked by dark sunglasses—hoping to blend in and be innocuous. Every so often he glanced impatiently at his watch. He was waiting for someone.

Just as he was beginning to suspect he was wasting his time, Fernando suddenly drifted along the sidewalk and coolly took a seat on the opposite end of the bench from Stirling, in a way that he hoped wouldn't draw suspicion. He was sweating, as always, but instead of his usual happy-go-lucky self, he seemed stressed out. Stirling hoped this wasn't a bad sign; he was depending on Fernando for information. He asked, "So what's the word, Nando?"

"I think I might have something that could help you."

Stirling closed and folded the newspaper. "Let's have it."

"Okay…there's a group of players who have been stirring up some trouble in and around the Yucatan."

"Where from?"

"Not sure. Maybe local, maybe not. But the point is they have a contact in Cuba who may have tipped them off on where to get C-4."

Stirling seemed a bit stunned at the revelation. "Interesting," he said. "How did you come across this information?"

Fernando was slightly flustered by the question. "What the fuck do you care? The lead is good. I'm telling you how it's linked to you. That's all that should matter, no?"

This wasn't the Fernando that Stirling was accustomed to. It wasn't like him to be so evasive, or to seem, well, scared. In a calm and soothing tone, Stirling said, "Go on."

"Anyway, the word from my lead is that these people are having a meet with some major player who may have been the provider of the C-4."

"Who is he?"

"No one really knows. But he's a man who always wears a white linen suit."

The absurdity of the description was not lost on Stirling. He tried to hold back laughter.

"A man in a white suit? Are you sure you don't mean a man in a gray flannel... Never mind."

Fernando wasn't well-versed with American and British postwar films; he might not even have heard of Alec Guinness or Gregory Peck, much less been familiar with the titles of their films, so the reference was lost on him. "Sorry," he said, with a confused look. "I don't understand..."

"Forget it. So what about this meeting?"

"The word is that it's going down Friday night, around midnight, at Luna Azul."

Stirling was familiar with the joint. He'd been there on a few occasions with Irina. He nodded and said, "So who's the group he's meeting with? What's the deal with them?"

Fernando shrugged his shoulders. "That's all I know, amigo. All I can tell you is, find the man in the white suit and you'll probably find the people who blew up your place."

Stirling believed the lead was solid. He would need to be there. "Thanks, Nando. I owe you."

As Stirling rose to leave, Fernando said, "Doc...you're going to need back up. You shouldn't go alone."

"No, Fernando. I don't want you there. This isn't your problem."

"I didn't mean me. But you know... I could maybe have one of my friends watch your back...just for safety. You never know..."

Stirling appreciated Fernando's concern. But nonetheless, he didn't want to involve him any more than necessary.

"No thanks, Nando. I'll go alone."

"Whatever you say. But, hey…it's one of my favorite Friday night hangouts, so you never know who you might run into, if you know what I mean."

The two men exchanged a knowing look. He was a character, Fernando, thought Stirling. "Just stay out of trouble," he said, with a note of concern.

"Always, Dr. Stirling. Always."

16

Literally translated, Luna Azul meant Blue Moon. Besides being the title of a song from 1934 that became a number one doo-wop hit for the Marcels in 1961, it was also the name of the most popular nightspot in Merida, located in an upscale area near Montecristo, where it catered mostly to tourists looking for a hot spot to party, dance, score, and hook-up. Friday nights were always packed, and this one was no exception. There were very special guests slated to arrive, and patrons lined up around the block.

Inside, bold vibrant colors coupled with an innovative sense of shape and design, made the nightspot appear like a cross between Roman Republic architecture and the Mos Eisley cantina of *Star Wars*—gaudy elegance coupled with vulgar extravagance—or like a Latin reincarnation of Studio 54. Like that long-ago famous NY hotspot, those lucky enough to be permitted admittance to Luna Azul left their inhibitions at the door. They ate, drank, smoked, snorted, and screwed from the bathroom stalls to the overhead catwalks. And some came to dance.

Because of its notoriety, it was always crawling with paparazzi, and photos from Blue Azul graced newspapers and tabloids all over the region. As such, it was a great place to be seen and be photographed and grab that five minutes of fame that just might be parlayed into five years' worth, and this is why Heidi Aronson, looking smashing as always with her form-fitting dress and stiletto heels, brought two of her newest Stun Agency discoveries to the club to introduce them to impolite society. They'd come to have a good time, to dance, and to be photographed in the company of the city's prominent movers and shakers.

There was extra excitement in the air tonight, as it was time for the club's monthly dance contest. Under the rules, seven couples could dance, in any style they wished, for a maximum of seven minutes. Runner-ups received 10,000 pesos; the winners got 25,000. Contestants showed off their moves on a circular dance floor. Tonight's theme was 1970s disco, and the entrants could choose any song from that era; the DJ was keeping the soundtrack to *Saturday Night Fever* in heavy rotation, currently playing the Bee Gees song "Night Fever" to a packed dance floor. Most everyone on the first floor was dressed in appropriate style for the disco era, with lots of shiny, form-fitting polyester, shirts and suit coats with wide collars, and stacked heels for both the men and the women.

The club was divided into three levels. The bottom floor had booths and tables situated around the perimeter of the dance floor, the middle level had wide catwalks leading to a round platform in the middle that supported an enormous circular bar, and the uppermost level—the most exclusive—had walkways around the outside perimeter wide enough to accommodate dining tables, with a large open space in the center that allowed the diners to literally look down on the dancers and less well-heeled patrons below.

Ernesto and Conseula sat in a third-level booth, their four bodyguards forming a perimeter around them as they welcomed their special guest for the evening, who sat directly across the round table from them. It was Ignacio, in a dark, sleek Italian suit that, with his hair tied back and clean-shaven, made him look like a model from the pages of GQ.

Next to him was an admirer, Rosy Calderon, one of Ernesto and Consuela's most dedicated and long-standing associates. A gorgeous Mexican woman made all the more alluring by the hint of a scar on her cheek—a reminder of a past assignment from which she barely escaped with her life—she was a skilled killer. Her cat-like eyes fixated on Ignacio. Maybe it was the mojitos, maybe just pure animal lust, but she wanted him. His poise, his quietness, his calm created a magnetic aura quite at odds with the frenetic atmosphere of the club. She wanted to dominate him, psychologically and sexually, and wipe that smug hint of a condescending smile off his handsome face.

For his part, Ignacio was polite—to be otherwise would be to insult his hosts—but he wasn't particularly impressed. Rosy was undeniably attractive, with her deep tan, full breasts, and hourglass figure. But he found women who were as brazenly sexually aggressive as she rather tawdry and unfeminine. He only fucked sluts like her when it was advantageous for him to do so. Or when he was desperate. Besides, he'd experienced the best sex of his life with Heidi, and when you've had haute cuisine, you lose your appetite for fast food.

Rosy knocked back the last sips of her drink in one gulp. Speaking loudly to be heard over the throbbing music, she said to Ignacio, "When this is over, let's you and me go fuck the night away."

She may as well have been talking to a wall; there was no reaction from Ignacio. He was surveying the others in the club, quickly assessing who might prove a threat. He wasn't looking at Rosy, and only knew she was speaking from Ernesto's stunned look and Consuela's shocked laugh.

"Rosy, my dear," said Ernesto, "if you want to have a conversation with Ignacio, you have to be sure he's facing you, so he can read your lips."

"You mean he's a dummy?"

"He's deaf, but he's no dummy."

Reading Ernesto's lips, Ignacio knew he'd just been insulted.

Rosy looked to Consuela, who nodded in confirmation, adding, "This is the most dangerous man you'll ever meet."

Rosy now looked at Ignacio, who had turned to face her, his face implacable, but a wicked gleam in his eye. He raised his glass to her, and gave her a slight bow of his head.

After years of working for Ernesto and Consuela, she knew Consuela to be a woman who was not easily impressed by anyone. This stoked the flame of her desire for Ignacio even more. She scooched closer to him, so her knee touched his. He didn't flinch a millimeter. Indeed, he reciprocated by pressing his knee against hers, and casually placed his hand on her bare thigh, which was peeking out from her slit-to-the-waist skirt. He gave her just the slightest hint of a smile as his hand squeezed her thigh, and she felt fireworks exploding up her spine. Just as she was about to mouth something very obscene to him, Ignacio turned his attention back to Ernesto.

"Whatever happens, we make this quick," said Ernesto. "He has to be taken out tonight. No questions asked. We have our orders."

Ignacio looked into Ernesto's eyes. He knew Ernesto and Consuela had no scruples. They would get the job done whatever the cost. To them, collateral damage was the price of doing business. To Ignacio, it was sloppy and unprofessional. He lived by an older code of gentlemen spies—go after your mark, but leave innocent civilians out of it. Ernesto and Consuela, on the other hand, lived by the code of the streets, where no one was innocent.

Below, on the first level, Heidi and her two newest recruits, Lidia and Sophia, sat at their table enjoying drinks and what Heidi affectionately termed "the freak show." The two eye-catching young women with her were not only the newest models for the Stun Agency, they were also socialites who often frequented the hottest nightspots in Merida, so Luna Azul was a familiar playground.

The mayor of Merida recognized Heidi and came over to greet her, kissing her hand. He also recognized Lidia and Sophia, whose parents were among his most faithful campaign donors. "You ladies found the right agency," he told them. "Before you know it, Heidi will have your faces on magazines all over the world."

As they continued making light banter, one of the many photographers in the club approached. Without hesitation, the mayor posed with the two lovely young women. The photo would certainly make the next day's papers, boosting both his image and theirs.

After the mayor went on his way, the ladies settled back in at their table. The dance contest would be starting soon. After it ended, they'd get out on the dance floor and celebrate their signing with the Stun Agency. "And," said Lidia, "you never know who you might hook up with."

Heidi just smiled. She wasn't interested in a casual hook-up. She'd just found someone she wanted to hold onto forever. And, unbeknownst to her, he was sitting just 400 feet away from her, two levels up.

It was about 11:30 when Stirling arrived and sauntered through the club's front door. In his blue silk shirt and black dress pants he looked elegant and immaculate. Though not exactly a young man, he was more fit and better-looking than most men half his age. No wonder that the women he strode past either followed him with their eyes or turned to get a second look. Stirling was unfazed; he was used to this kind of attention, and felt it was mostly shallow and unwarranted.

The dance contest was just beginning, the first entrants doing an energetic tango-inspired dance to the Trammps' "Disco Inferno." Stirling wound his way around to one of the few empty tables and sat down. Catching the eye of a mini-skirted waitress, he waved her over and ordered a beer.

Sitting a few tables away from Stirling, Lidia and Sophia noticed him and pointed him out to Heidi. "How is that guy alone?" asked Lidia.

"He won't be, by the end of the evening," said Sophia, staking her claim.

Heidi laughed. "Don't waste your time. I know him."

"Is he gay?" asked Sophia.

"No, but he's spoken for."

"Then what's he doing here?"

Up on the second level, Fernando had spotted Stirling entering the club and took note of where he was now sitting. He'd done his job. Now he just needed to collect his pay. Trying to be inconspicuous, he wormed his way through the crowd and trod up the steps to the next level. He heard the Master of Ceremonies below introduce the next couple, who would be dancing to Yvonne Elliman's "If I Can't Have You," and looked around until he saw a booth with four beefy men standing around it, looking outward. Bingo.

He ambled to the booth. As he approached, Ernesto stood to give him a bear hug, as if they were lifelong friends. "So wonderful to see you, Fernando," said Ernesto.

"Yes, it's been far too long," agreed Consuela, offering her hand, which Fernando kissed politely and held.

"Good to see you both," replied Fernando, with a nervous grin. His gaze fell on Rosy, who gave him an inviting smile, those beguiling cat-like eyes working their magic. He was thunderstruck.

"So what about our man?" asked Consuela.

"Yes," said Ernesto, "is he in town?"

"Better," said Fernando. "He's here."

Ignacio, reading the conversation on the conspirators' lips, leaned forward.

"Really?" said Consuela. She and Ernesto were surprised but pleased; Fernando had exceeded their meager expectations.

"How did you manage it?" asked Ernesto.

"Easy," said Fernando. "He trusts me."

Ignacio read the betrayal on Fernando's lips. It repulsed him. He had little use for people who treated loyalty like a commodity, for sale to the highest bidder. He found it not only distasteful but pathetic.

"His loss," said Ernesto.

Consuela rose from the booth and moved to the rail. "Where is he?" she asked.

Ernesto joined her, stepping beside her. Fernando came up behind them. "Bottom floor. Blue shirt. Just… there."

He casually pointed in Stirling's direction. Consuela caught sight of him; she knew what he looked like from his photograph. She gave a satisfied nod.

Ernesto patted Fernando's shoulder. "My friend, you do not disappoint."

"So I—I can have my money now?" Fernando asked, his voice tremulously.

"Indeed," said Consuela, "you deserve what's coming to you."

"And a bonus," said Ernesto. He looked back at Rosy and gave a sharp nod of his head toward Fernando. She rose slowly and sauntered over to Fernando, her shapely hips swaying. He watched her approach with breathless anticipation.

Reaching him, she took his sweaty hand in hers and said, in a breathy voice, "Come with me."

He planned on doing exactly that.

Stirling was restless. Nursing his beer, he kept scanning the crowd. The dance contest was in full swing, the crowd clapping and cheering the contestants, some of whom were clearly ringers from the local dance studios. The third couple was just finishing a sort of interpretive dance to KC and the Sunshine Band's "Boogie Shoes," and so far, the only man Stirling had seen wearing a white suit was a John Travolta-wannabe too wet-behind-the-ears to be a trained killer. Looking around, he saw what appeared to be a door leading to an outdoor patio on the second level. Perhaps his man was there. He began making his way to the stairs.

Standing at the third floor rail up above, Esteban, one of Ernesto and Consuela's men, turned to his bosses and said, "He's making a move."

Ernesto turned to another bodyguard and said, "Julio, go with Esteban and greet our friend."

Rosy burst into the ladies' room holding Fernando's hand, dragging him along behind her. The bathroom was huge, with about twenty-five stalls and a few women standing at the washbasins who were either too drunk or too stoned to either notice or care. Fernando heard moaning coming from one stall, whose door rattled as the woman inside, her back pressed against it, was fucked by an eager, panting man. Just another Friday at Luna Azul…

Rosy took him to an empty stall on the end of the row and playfully pushed him inside. She stepped in after him and latched the door. Fernando was already bulging in anticipation, eyes wide, a leering grin on his face. Rosy pushed him down onto the closed toilet seat straddled his lap, grabbed his head between her hands and shoved her tongue down his throat, kissing him furiously.

The thrumming music continued filtering in from the dance floor; now it was Donna Summer's "I Feel Love."

Rosy stuck her tongue in Fernando's ear. He shuddered, and his hands began clawing madly at his belt, clumsily unbuckling it. Then he unbuttoned and unzipped his pants, trembling in hungry anticipation.

Rosy pulled back, gently caressed his cheeks, and cooed, "Whoa, cowboy. Slow down. Let's make this memorable." Fernando paused, chastised. She gave him a devilish grin, reached behind her neck, and deftly unclasped the straps of her gown. She slowly pulled them forward and downward, revealing curvaceous tanned breasts with erect brown nipples, aureoles as big as silver dollars.

Fernando almost fainted. "Sweet Jesus!" he whispered.

Cupping her hands beneath her breasts, Rosy offered them up to his slavering mouth. "That's it, baby," she breathed. His hand glided up her soft, warm thigh, and he was delighted to discover she wasn't wearing any panties. She purred, "Yes, darling. That's it." Her fingers wrapped around his bulging shaft, her thumb massaging the tip. He made a little sound, almost like a whimper.

She whispered into his ear, "Just let me get out of this dress and, I swear, you'll never have another night like this."

Stirling emerged onto the patio to find it deserted; everyone was watching the dance contest. Still, he was grateful for the cool night air, so refreshing after the pungent stew of odors inside, equal parts sweat, cologne, perfume, and desperation. He looked out at the Merida skyline, bathed in the blue light of a full moon.

He wondered if Fernando had led him on a wild goose chase. It seemed apparent there was no man in a white suit. And if Fernando had lied about that, what else might he have lied about? He felt a crushing disappointment. In the old days, he wouldn't have given his trust so easily to someone so questionably deserving. He was losing his edge. And this was no time to—

He heard footsteps behind him, and knew what to expect even before he turned around to see Julio and Esteban. "Good evening, gentlemen," said Stirling, trying to appear calm even as his mind raced.

Neither Julio nor Esteban said a word.

"Nice night," continued Stirling.

They remained motionless and silent, but only for a moment. And then Julio whipped out a knife from a sheath on the back of his belt and lunged for Stirling.

Stirling defected the blow with a beer bottle, then smashed it against Julio's ear. The bottle broke, leaving Stirling holding the jagged-edged neck. As Esteban lunged, Stirling sidestepped and swung the bottle. He felt it catch soft flesh, and saw Esteban fall grasping his neck, a gaping wound across his jugular gushing blood.

Seeing his partner dying in front of him, Julio went into a fury. He again lunged at Stirling, this time nicking his bicep, despite Stirling's effort to evade him. They faced off, moving in a circle, each one waiting for the other to make a move. Stirling paused in front of a table. He made a feint at Julio, and Julio reacted, lunging again with the knife. Stirling leapt aside, and Julio's knife embedded into the polished wood of the tabletop. He tried to pull it out. It was stuck. He spun around just as Stirling caught him with a karate chop to the throat.

But Julio was tough. Gagging and coughing, he threw punches at Stirling, who returned as good as he got. Julio was a skilled fighter, moving quickly, but the throat punch had taken some of the wind out of his sails—enough for Stirling, older and rustier, to get an edge.

The hits were hard and brutal. Punches to the midsection. Elbows to the face. Stirling took the upper hand by grabbing Julio's forearm and flipping him over his shoulder. Julio's firm, powerful body smashed onto the patio like a boulder. But as Stirling leapt forward, Julio landed a strong side-kick to Stirling's face which sent him reeling backward, smashing into and overturning another table. Both men were winded now. As Julio leapt for him, Stirling swung with a hard right. Julio quickly ducked and returned the favor with a sharp left to the solar plexus. Stirling hunched over, grabbing his midsection.

He looked up to see Julio tugging at the knife embedded in the table. And it was beginning to come loose. This had to end. Now.

Stirling leapt onto Julio's back, his arms curling under Julio's armpits, his hands locking behind Julio's neck. He had him in an unbreakable chokehold, though Julio did try to escape by propelling himself backwards. They both fell onto the patio, Julio landing atop Stirling, but Stirling didn't release his grip. He grimaced, pushing his interlocked hands forward as Julio did his best to shove his head backwards. But Stirling had the momentum.

There was a loud snap.

Julio went limp.

And Stirling slowly rose to his feet. He hated having to kill Julio, though he knew if he hadn't, Julio would surely have killed him. But Stirling was a man dedicated to saving lives, not taking them. Not anymore. Not until now.

He could hear the music from inside the club. Thelma Houston. "Don't Leave Me This Way."

He did a quick self-inspection. There was a smudge of Esteban's blood on his shirt, but in the dim light of the club, the wet red blood might not be so noticeable on his dark blue shirt. He needed to leave. And he needed to find Fernando, and get some answers.

On the dance floor, the next contestants launched into an energetic, acrobatic dance to the Bee Gees' "Stayin' Alive." The distinctive guitar chords filtered into the ladies' room, where Fernando was astride the blood-spattered toilet, his pants around his ankles, his head tilted back against the wall, his dismembered member in his mouth, and thirty silver Libertad coins scattered on the bloody floor around him.

At the washbasin, Rosy rinsed her hands, wiped some spots of blood off her cheeks, checked to make sure there were no bloodstains on her clothes, and left. She passed a young girl who was heading to the bathroom, and as she started up the stairs, she heard a faint scream.

Ernesto and Consuela looked up as Rosy approached their table.

"Well?" asked Consuela. "Did he get his reward?"

"Absolutely," said Rosy, reclaiming her seat next to Ignacio. "Left him speechless, and feeling awfully full of himself."

Ignacio caught enough of this exchange to be disgusted by it, and by the speck of blood in the dark hair behind Rosy's left ear.

Ignacio stood and went to the rail, where one of the bodyguards, Rafael, was looking for signs of Julio and Esteban. They'd been gone just long enough for it to be worrisome.

Down below, the dance contest was winding down. The disco music was infectious, and as the contest progressed, more and more of the watchers on the sidelines were getting into the groove, doing their own moves to the upbeat music. And now, as the next-to-last couple took the floor to Michael Jackson's "Don't Stop Til You Get Enough," Ignacio saw a familiar face in the crowd—Heidi, laughing and dancing with her two new models. Lost in the music, she threw her head back, moving to the rhythm. And then she saw him, looking down on her, and her face beamed with an excited smile. She waved at Ignacio. He smiled, and waved back. She motioned for him to come down and join her.

Ignacio turned to his hosts, excused himself, and moved to the staircase. He needed to at least say hello to Heidi. Perhaps they could arrange to see each other later. He noticed a young woman down below who, in contrast to the ecstatic dancers on the main floor, appeared to be scared and crying. She led a security guard towards the bathroom.

At the same moment, the second-floor patio door opened and Stirling stepped onto the catwalk. Ignacio watched as he began pushing through the crowd, making his way to the stairs.

Rafael, still stationed at the third floor rail, spotted him and spun back to Ernesto and Consuela. "It's him! The doctor!"

Ernesto was shocked. He and Consuela exchanged a look that spoke volumes. If Stirling was leaving the club, that meant Julio and Esteban had failed, and were likely dead. But he'd come to Luna Azul with a Plan B—Rafael and Gustavo, his remaining bodyguards, both wore loose-fitting black jackets over their muscled bodies, the better to hide the compact MAC-10 machine pistols tucked away in their shoulder holsters. They were crude, nasty guns, capable of firing all 32 rounds in their magazines in seconds. They weren't terribly accurate for target shooting, but in a large public place such as this, they could inflict horrible carnage. And that's exactly what Ernesto wanted. Mayhem. He'd hide the hit in a massacre.

With a scowl, Ernesto commanded, "Kill 'em all!"

Gustavo and Rafael unholstered their weapons and opened fire. Each had multiple clips in their coat pockets and attached to their belts. They'd empty one, pop it out, slap another in, and keep firing. They had a practiced rhythm going—one fired while the other reloaded. 9MM firepower sprayed throughout the club. The roar of the guns firing was deafening, especially after the DJ ducked for cover, bullets striking his turntable. The patrons screamed, dove under tables, and swarmed to the exits.

Still on the second level, Ignacio briefly locked eyes with Heidi. He frantically motioned for her to get down. He was torn—should he run to protect her, or go back and disarm the gunmen? The latter was out of the question; the throngs of panicked people shoving forward en masse pushed him toward the stair to the first floor. It was all he do to remain standing. Some people didn't, and were trampled underfoot.

Stirling had already reached the ground floor. He saw a young couple in front of him, the man bleeding from a head wound, the woman trying to get him to his feet. They were about to be stampeded. As he reached them, he grabbed the man's arm, pulled it around his shoulder, and lifted him up. The three of them made a bee-line for a side exit.

All around them, people were being struck by the bee swarm bursts of gunfire. Many were hit, some fatally wounded. Glass shattered. Lights sparked. Grey smoke hung like a fog over the third level, and the acrid smell of gunpowder filled the club, along with gunshots and screams.

Ignacio made his way to the stairwell, climbed over it, and dropped to the first floor. He rushed to where he'd last seen Heidi, and saw her on the floor, laying on her right side behind an overturned table. Her friends were gone, having raced out to escape the pandemonium. Rushing to Heidi's side, Ignacio knelt beside her. Blood pooled beneath her head, but she appeared to be breathing. He cradled her shoulders and lifted her up to his lap. Her head lolled back, and he saw that one of the bullets had struck the back of her skull and the concussion had blasted out the right cheek of the face that had once graced magazine covers from Manhattan to Madrid.

Her one good eye moved, slowly, and he knew she recognized him. Despite the burning pain in her head, she was comforted by his presence. To her, he looked just like an angel. And that was her last thought before all went black. Ignacio saw the light fade from her eyes, and he knew she was gone.

He immediately felt white-hot rage.

The gunfire ceased, replaced by the terrified screams and wails of those who'd seen their loved ones murdered in front of their eyes. Panicked people still crowded around the exits, trying to leave the club.

Ignacio left Heidi and dashed to the stairs. He took them three at a time as he raced back to the third level, where he intended to tear the gunmen to pieces. But when he arrived, there was no one there. Ernesto, Consuela, Rosy, and the bodyguards had escaped.

Ignacio's thoughts were a jumble; he wanted to stay by Heidi, but he knew he couldn't. He became aware of something he hadn't felt since he was a child. Tears. His own hot tears, streaming down his cheeks. He wept. And wailed, an agonized sound. Inside him was a well of emptiness, quickly filling with hate. Wiping his eyes, he saw red and blue lights flashing across the bullet-riddled, blood-stained walls. Police were approaching. He needed to disappear.

He quickly exited the building, stepping over the dead and dying, and dashed to his car. He pulled into traffic just as the police cars and emergency vehicles arrived at the club.

So senseless, so stupid, he thought. And why her? Why had he lost the one woman he'd ever met who managed to touch his heart?

He wanted to punish those who'd taken her. The bodyguards. Ernesto. Consuela. And the reason they were at the club in the first place—Dr. Kent Stirling.

17

The road to Progreso was virtually empty, so Stirling drove his BMW at a fast pace. It was just after two in the morning. The sudden explosion of violence at the nightclub left him amped up, adrenaline pumping, his mind racing. Discipline, he thought to himself. Breathe. Get a grip. If he was the target, why the indiscriminate shooting? Who would want him dead, and why kill so many innocents in trying to take him out?

It had to be the Sandbox. But why, after so much time had passed? And why now? All he knew for certain was that Gavin Weller was the man behind the curtain. The man who'd sent assassins to take him out. He could still hear the sickening sound of Julio's neck snapping, followed by the gunfire, the sound of bodies pierced by hot lead, the screams of the helpless. He couldn't shake it. And he couldn't let it go unanswered.

Too many friends and loved ones had died doing the Sandbox's bidding. And now the ones still alive were being terminated. He was definitely on the list, and now many innocent civilians had lost their lives just for being in the wrong place, a place where the Sandbox had lured him.

Dr. Kent Stirling, skilled surgeon, dedicated to saving lives, died that night.

Kent Stirling, cold-blooded assassin for the Sandbox, remorseless taker of lives, resurrected.

Ariel Manzanero's stomach turned as he surveyed the aftermath of the violence at Luna Azul. The inside was practically demolished, a scene of carnage unlike anything he'd ever witnessed. The floor was covered with shattered glass, shattered bodies, pools of blood, and spent shell casings. This was the kind of case that could make a detective, put him in the forefront of a lurid story that would be reported and analyzed by news outlets and tabloids for months, even years, to come. And here he'd thought he'd have a quiet retirement and disappear into a low-key life whose highlight would be fishing with his grandkids.

Instead he was surrounded by death. Senseless, violent, wasteful death. He stepped slowly among the bodies on the first floor and saw Heidi Aronson, whom he recognized and knew to be a local celebrity, though he'd never actually spoken to her, and now he never would. Ariel Manzanero was sworn to protect his community's citizens. But that night, as far as he was concerned, he had failed them. The loss was palpable. How many sons and daughters and mothers and fathers of Merida had left their homes that night looking forward to a fun time only to meet a horrible end?

The question plagued him as he ascended the stairs to the second floor, where two suspected gangsters lay dead on the balcony, and then the third, where a man known to have been a low-life informer had been gruesomely killed in a ladies' room stall. How the hell was all this connected?

Two things he knew, or at least suspected very strongly, in that moment. One was that his friend Kent Stirling was somehow at the middle of it. Two was that by morning, the chiefs above him would clamp down on the media and make sure it was reported as a massacre perpetrated by the dead goons on the second-floor patio, to protect the not-so-innocent.

Stirling returned to his beachfront home in Progreso. He entered cautiously, going room to room to be certain he was alone. Then he took a shower, attempting to wash away the dread and paranoia that now coursed through him. Slipping into a bathrobe, he went to his study and poured himself a brandy. As he sat in the dim light and sipped his drink, his thoughts turned to Irina. Thank God she hadn't been with him, having gone to Veracruz for a few days to visit her grandmother. This would give him some time to think about the situation he now found himself in. He knew she would be back soon enough, and he didn't want her getting caught in the crossfire. He'd never forgive himself if something happened to her.

He pulled his cell phone from the pocket of his robe and dialed a number. The phone rang twice on the other end before being answered.

"Young here." Evan Young tried to stifle the yawn that escaped as he spoke his name, but wasn't entirely successful. He'd been awakened in the middle of the night by his buzzing cell phone.

"Evan, it's Kent Stirling."

Young quickly sat up and dialed the security code into the phone, sweeping the line.

"The line's clean," said Young. "Go ahead."

"Evan, they fucking did it again."

"Who did what again?"

"The Sandbox tried to take me out again! Pulled no punches. Had a hit squad tail me to a nightclub and just… opened fire." Stirling could hardly believe it himself, even as he said it. Even having been there. He was generally able to control his emotions and keep them in check, but not tonight.

"Which club?"

"What the hell difference does that make?"

"Kent, I need fucking information. I need you to give me as many facts as possible. Otherwise, I can't help you."

Stirling closed his eyes and held the phone away. They were both stressed, but he felt he could trust Young. There was no one else. He needed inside information from someone with ties to the Sandbox. He put the phone back to his ear and continued, "A place called Luna Azul. About thirty miles outside of central Merida. I'm sure it'll be all over the news this morning."

Young quickly jotted down notes on a small steno pad. "What about you... are you injured?"

"No, but…Evan, I…I killed two men."

Young paused. He inhaled nervously. Having been Stirling's handler back in the day, he knew what this meant. He'd trained Stirling, and even worked with him in the field. And he knew how hard Stirling had worked to leave that world behind, and free himself from the demands of the Sandbox. Hearing this admission from Stirling was like hearing a lethal weapon being unsheathed from its holster. "Any idea who they were?" he asked.

Stirling thought for a moment, recalling their scowling faces. "No..." he sighed. "I'd never seen either of them before." After a moment, he added, "Evan…there's one thing you should probably know. Hell, I have no idea at this point. Maybe you know what this means because I got nothing out of it."

"What is it?"

"I have a contact here named Fernando. His information led me to that club. He said that the shooters were going to have a meet with a man in a white linen suit."

Young sat up; this hit a nerve. "Kent..." he said with concern, "you need to come in as soon as possible. I may have a lead on this."

"You know who this character is?"

"No one I know has ever actually seen him, but he played a part in the Italian Operation that caused that whole debacle years ago."

"I remember. But I can't leave here."

"Kent, I'm telling you—I don't think it's safe for you there anymore. Not in the Yucatan and not in Belize. Come in and we'll go after these people together. There's still time."

"No!" Stirling barked adamantly. "My days of playing cloak and dagger are over. Evan, don't take offense to what

I'm going to tell you, but these fuckers brought this fight to my doorstep, and I'll be damned if I'm going to let them run me out of here. This is my home. I have a life here. Do you understand me?"

"Had a life," Young said matter-of-factly. "Do you understand me?" There was a long pause on the other end of the line. Young knew he'd hit a raw nerve. And he also knew he wouldn't convince Stirling to come back, but he couldn't remain in the Yucatan.

"I'm sorry, Kent. What are you going to do?"

Stirling let out a defeated sigh. "What can I do? Lay low for a while. See what I can find out here on my own. Maybe I can bring them out in the open if I keep myself in the general area. Evan—call me if you find out anything. You know where to find me."

Young nodded affirmatively. "Take care, old friend."

"You do the same."

Young clicked off the call. He rose from his bed and paced to the window. Looking into the darkness, he dialed another number. The phone was answered on the first ring. A woman's voice said, "Yes?"

"This is Young. Get me Gavin Weller."

Ariel Manzanero and his team carefully sifted through the evidence at Luna Azul. Assisting them was a forensics team that included Yvette Cruz, a brilliant young specialist who'd proven herself in three previous cases where her keen eye for detail helped Manzanero take down local crime rings. Mid-thirties, with green eyes and shoulder-length light brown hair tied back, Cruz wore virtually no make-up, but didn't have to. She was naturally attractive, originally from the city of Cancun, and spoke perfect English.

Cruz spotted something in the wall by the main bar on the second level. It was a shell casing from one of the bullets. As she examined it closely with tweezers, Manzanero approached her. He asked, "What have you got?"

"Shell casing from a 9mm bullet. But in all my time doing this job, I've never seen one like this in any part of Mexico."

"What's so special about it?"

She brought it under the hard light from the ceiling bulbs so they could examine it together. "This is a Glaser Safety Slug."

"Never heard of it."

"Because they're not popular in this part of the world. They're basically supercharged hollow point bullets."

"I don't follow."

"They're filled with No. 12 birdshot with a flat polymer cap that improves its ballistic performance."

Manzanero nodded, impressed by her expert knowledge. "Meaning?"

She continued, "Meaning the projectile in the cartridge is much more lightweight than conventional cartridges. Exits the bore at a significantly higher muzzle velocity. Causes a large shallow wound, and because it's extremely lightweight and fragile, it's viciously lethal, like being hit with miniature rounds of buckshot. Guaranteed death if they hit you in the right spot. No chance of surviving."

Manzanero nodded, impressed with her as always. "Great work, Cruz."

"Thank you," she said. She scanned the room. The deceased had now been taken away, the locations of their bodies temporarily memorialized by white tape silhouettes and pools of dried blood. Crime scene photographers snapped photos while other techs collected evidence throughout the three levels of the club.

"Trouble here isn't a lack of evidence," she said. "It's that there's too much."

Manzanero sighed, "Maybe that was the intention."

18

The warm sun shone down on the mourners assembled at Merida Central Cemetery. They gathered, friends and family, to pay their last respects to Heidi Aronson. That she had been well-loved in the community was evidenced by the size of the crowd congregating at the gravesite, after the in-church service. Ignacio had not attended the services, but he did come to pay his last respects to Heidi, pretending to be visiting another gravesite a good distance away, in the shadow of an oak tree. He wasn't alone. There were a number of others in the cemetery that day, saying final goodbyes; the days following the Merida Massacre, as the press dubbed it, were filled with funerals.

Wearing a black suit and sunglasses and holding a single white orchid, Ignacio waited patiently as the priest and mourners said their farewells and dispersed, and the grave was covered over. There was no headstone just yet, but the flowers from the funeral service were placed at the head of Heidi's burial site. When everyone was gone, he walked to the fresh grave, placed the white orchid atop it, and signed a farewell—"Goodbye, my dear one."

He had no tears for Heidi. He had already grieved for her, spending a day in the darkness of his hotel room considering his life, the path it had taken, and how much it had cost him. He'd never been terribly introspective before; he considered himself an instrument, doing the bidding of others for a handsome price. That shielded him from thinking about the consequences of his actions. But Heidi had touched him, lit a spark in his heart that he thought had long ago gone cold as ice. He'd only had a fraction of time with her, but it was enough to fracture him, to pierce his carefully managed façade. He knew he'd never meet anyone else like her, not for the rest of his days.

And he promised he would avenge her.

At Progreso Beach, parasailing boats glided over the surf, tourists worked on their suntans, locals bathed in the warm azure sea, and the elite cruised the coastline in their incredibly expensive yachts. Even after several days, the nightclub massacre was a highlight of the local news, and for one 24-hour news cycle had received international coverage, but it was quickly supplanted by stories of political misdeeds, faraway wars, and a feel-good incident involving a hiker who fell into a ravine and languished for a day before his hiking companion—his pet bulldog—managed to alert rescuers. The shootings at the nightclub were a tragedy, to be sure, but now that most of the deceased had been lain to rest, life went on.

Since the accident, Dr. Kent Stirling had cut back drastically on his appointments, so Olivia found herself with little to do except catch up on paperwork—of which there was very little, owing to her diligence and efficiency—and to finally indulge in books she'd been longing to read. But today was the end of the month, a time she always set aside for bookkeeping, making sure all invoices were input into the computer billing system, and prioritizing unpaid accounts that would need to be followed up on. It was her least favorite part of her job, a pain in the ass, but a necessary evil. Someone had to do it.

She sat at her desk, going through the mind-numbing drudgery, trying not to be too distracted by Lola, laying on the floor near her feet. Even the little dog seemed bored, its usually bright, excited eyes, so much like a human's, at half-mast. She occasionally drifted into sleep and interspersed her snoring with little yips. She must be dreaming, Olivia imagined. She mused about what a dog's dream must be; was she leaping and bounding through an endless lawn, her silvery sandalwood hair wafted by a gentle breeze, chasing birds and rabbits, or was Olivia part of Lola's dream, tossing endless tennis balls for Lola to chase?

Damnit—she'd lost her place. Did she enter this invoice already? She'd have to backtrack and double-check. Maybe if she took a moment to breathe and get re-oriented, she'd be better able to maintain her focus. She sat back in her chair, closed her eyes, and took a deep breath. Let it out slowly. Listened to the Angela Aguilar song playing softly over the office stereo system. And then Lola emitted a faint growl.

Olivia opened her eyes and saw the Silky Terrier now on its feet, alerting. Something was off. Lola sensed it, and so now did Olivia. Lola growled more loudly. "Lola," said Olivia, "what is it?" She picked up the remote for the stereo and clicked a button to shut it off. Listened intently for any sound. Lola took a few steps toward the hallway and barked loudly as a shadow flitted across the open doorway.

"We're closed!" shouted Olivia. Her voice registered her fear. She heard footsteps in the hallway. There was more growling and barking from Lola, who stood in front of Olivia to protect her. And then Olivia saw him—a man of about 50, dressed wretchedly in torn jeans and a stained wife-beater undershirt, over which was a leather bomber jacket. The man's hair was unkempt, face unshaven, eyebrows dark and thick, and when he smiled, his misaligned grey-and-yellow teeth, with one incisor chipped, made him look malevolent.

The man grunted, "I have an appointment."

Olivia cringed as the man came through the doorway and moved slowly forward. His hands dangled at his sides, the fingers of his big mitts slightly curled inward, as if they were already practicing the best way to strangle her. Lola kept up her barking and growling, but backed up a few steps towards Olivia, who asked, trying to sound neutral, "Who are you?"

"Ladrillo," said the man. When translated, the name meant 'brick.' He stood still and took a long, admiring look at

Olivia, taking in her long dark hair, short skit, and form-fitting blouse.

Olivia backed into her desk. "You must be mistaken," she said. "We have no appointments today."

"I didn't mean that you have an appointment for me," Ladrillo said in a voice that sounded like someone had sandpapered his windpipe. "I have one with you."

Lola stopped barking and shot to Ladrillo, biting at his heels and ankles. Ladrillo kicked backwards, sending the little dog rolling. Coming up on her feet, Lola yelped, and began an incessant barrage of barking. Ladrillo casually reached into his bomber jacket and pulled out a silenced 9mm pistol.

"No!" screamed Olivia, as Ladrillo pointed the gun at Lola. With all her might, Olivia threw her weight onto his gun arm, pulling it down as he pulled the trigger. He got off three quick shots, splintering the floor and the plaster of the wall inches away from Lola. Frightened, the little dog spun and dashed out the door, heading for the steps.

Ladrillo chuckled. "Your protector?" he said with a grin, nodding towards the still-open door, where Lola's barking became fainter as she skittered away.

Alone now, a chill shuddered through Olivia's body. She braced for the worst. And here it came…

Ladrillo lunged at her. One meaty hand clamped around her throat and slammed her backwards onto her desk. Grinning and gurgling a crazed laugh, Ladrillo placed the pistol on the corner of the desk and, his free hand now empty, began tugging at her blouse. She fought back, punching and slapping. He seemed to enjoy it. She grabbed a fistful of his greasy hair and yanked. He slapped her forearm hard enough that she let go. But then she dug in her fingernails near his eyes.

Now the fun and games were over. He punched her. Time to finish it. But before he did, he'd have his way with her, show her who was boss.

Lola dashed to a house down the street from the clinic. She saw Reynaldo on his front lawn, reclining in a lounge chair, reading a newspaper. She went to him, barking non-stop. Reynaldo lowered his paper and glanced at her.

"What is it, little one?" he asked. "Why are you making such a racket?"

Sensing something was off, he swung his legs over the side of the lounge chair. Lola ran a short distance toward the clinic, looked back at Reynaldo, and began barking again.

"Something wrong?" he queried. She ran toward him, barking, then spun and headed back toward the clinic. Reynaldo thought maybe the dog was trying to tell him something. He rose to his feet and trotted after her.

Reynaldo followed Lola up the steps to the second-floor clinic, both quiet as they came stealthily to the door. He entered to see Ladrillo, still with one hand pressing down on Olivia's throat, his other hand ripping off her blouse before tugging at her skirt.

Reacting quickly, adrenaline pumping, Reynaldo lifted up a wooden chair from the waiting area, ran forward, and slammed it against Ladrillo's back, but he lost his grip on it in the process. It dropped to the floor. Enraged at being interrupted, Ladrillo spun around, temporarily releasing Olivia, so he could pound in the face of this old man. As he pulled his fist back to do so, there was a silenced bang. Olivia had snatched his pistol up from the corner of the desk, pressed it into his back, and pulled the trigger. The bullet passed through his heart and exited his chest, barely missing Reynaldo.

Ladrillo looked down at the red bloom spreading across his wife-beater undershirt. He grunted, astounded at this turn of events, and then stumbled toward the window. Again picking up the chair, Reynaldo growled and charged into Ladrillo, slamming the chair, legs first, into him. The bleeding man fell back against the window and crashed through it. He dropped like a bag of cement to the asphalt of the patio, his neck snapping like a twig on impact.

Olivia tried to pull herself together, but couldn't help crying, both from fear of the situation she was just in and from relief. Reynaldo snatched up a blanket that was covering a sofa and draped it over Olivia's shoulders. She was like a daughter to him; he hated to see her shamed and humiliated. She hugged Reynaldo, wiping her tears.

"It's alright, my dead," said Reynaldo. "It's over." Lola, at Olivia's feet, let out a little bark. Reynaldo lifted the dog up to Olivia, and she took it in her arms, hugging it close. "I love you, you smart little doggie," Olivia cooed, giving Lola a kiss.

"Come on," said Reynaldo. "Let's go someplace safe.

Reynaldo walked Olivia and Lola next door to his home. As soon as they entered, he found a shirt for her to put on, to replace her torn blouse. He then called Stirling and told him to come immediately. Making tea for Olivia, he sat with her at his kitchen table, keeping quiet, allowing her to process what had just happened. She just held Lola close, caressing and petting her, with a faraway look in her eyes.

Soon, they heard the screech of car tires. Looking out his window, Reynaldo saw Stirling's car whip around the corner and come to a quick, lurching stop in front of his house. Stirling practically leapt out of the car and came bounding up to the front door. He was just about to ring the bell when Reynaldo opened it, quickly closing it after Stirling entered.

Seeing Stirling, Olivia rose from her chair and ran to his arms. He hugged her tightly, saying, "It's alright. I'm here now... I'm here."

"Kent... I'm sorry," she sobbed. "I should have kept the door locked. I had no idea."

"Don't worry, dear. You did nothing wrong. There was no way of knowing."

Reynaldo was reluctant to put in his two cents, but knew they might all be in danger. Coming up behind them, he put his hand on Stirling's shoulder and squeezed it. "Stirling...?"

Stirling turned to him, saying, "I'm sorry you got involved with all this. Are you alright?"

"I'm fine. But this man... neither of us ever saw him before." Reynaldo looked down at Lola, who was at Stirling and Olivia's feet. "You know," he said, "if it hadn't been for this little one, we might not have been so lucky."

Tears in her eyes, Olivia scooped up her precious pooch. Stirling petted the dog's head. "Good girl, Lola," he said. Then he looked into Olivia's eyes. She was shaken, but she was a strong woman. She'd get past this. He leaned forward and kissed her forehead. She touched his cheek. She appreciated his strength. She needed it. For the first time since the gunman had entered their office, she felt safe.

They heard sirens approaching. It was a combination of police vehicles and a coroner's wagon, come to collect the dead body. Stirling went out to talk to them and explained that his assistant had been attacked. Olivia gave a statement Stirling had practiced with her, saying that a crazed man had come into the office looking for drugs and tried to rape her, and Reynaldo had struggled with him. Reynaldo backed up both their accounts.

Stirling had standing in the community, and so, he suspected, did the people who'd sent the gunman. Payoffs would be made; the investigation would be a cursory one and the incident soon swept under the rug.

After the police left, Reynaldo poured his friend a drink. He could see that Stirling, while trying to project a calm demeanor, was fuming inside. His patience was at its limit. He'd never wanted to put his friends or loved ones in any jeopardy. Apparently, having failed to get him, his enemies had gone after someone close to him. The battle lines were drawn, and it was clear they were taking no prisoners.

After downing his drink and assuring himself that Olivia was okay, Stirling headed for the door, saying to her, "Call me before you leave tonight, and call me again when you get home. I won't sleep unless I know you're safe. Understood?"

She nodded.

"You, too, Reynaldo. Check in with me later."

"I will," agreed Reynaldo.

"Where are you going?" asked Olivia.

But Stirling said nothing as he stepped quietly out the door. He already knew the truth. This wasn't just some random gunman. This was the work of the Sandbox. And he wanted the man pulling the gunman's strings.

He wanted Gavin Weller.

A black Mercedes cruised quietly down the main highway from Progreso to Merida. Leaving the main drag, it maneuvered along the dirt side roads leading to a secluded area in the swamplands. Flamingos ran and flew off in the distance as the car approached their territory. The car's engine shut off and it coasted down a slight incline to a spot with the river on one side and tall grass and watery marshes on the other.

The car pulled to the side of the road and then turned, on a downward slope, facing the swamp. It stopped. The windows glided down. Inside was Ignacio. The car was meant to be a bonus given to him in advance for the completion of his mission. But now it was a reminder of an associated he abhorred. His rage over the killing of Heidi Aronson ran deep. She was dead. The Sandbox was responsible.

He wanted nothing to do with the Sandbox ever again.

And he wanted no reminders of them.

He stepped out of the car and walked forward. Picking up a rock, he tossed it into the water below. It made a satisfying plop; it seemed deep enough.

He got into the car and placed the gear in neutral. Stepping out, he went to the back, put both hands against the trunk, and gave it a good shove. It began to roll forward, picking up momentum as it coasted down the slope and into the swamp. He watched it sink, the back upending, the dark water seeming to boil around it as the air inside was displaced.

He stood there for a few minutes, watching and waiting for it to sink completely to the bottom of the murky depths. It didn't take long for the car to disappear, leaving behind a few bubbles rising to the surface.

Ignacio removed his sunglasses from the breast pocket of his coat and slipped them on. Stepping back up to the road, he walked steadily along, watching flamingos ahead of him fly up into the salmon-colored sky. This area, between the cities, belonged to nature, where underneath the serenity of the surface, survival of the fittest was the rule.

He would take that aspect of nature back to the city.

On the main highway, he walked a short distance until he saw a cab without a fare approaching. He waved his arm and flagged it down. The taxi stopped and Ignacio stepped inside. It didn't take the cabbie long to realize that his passenger was mute. But Ignacio had no trouble indicating where he wanted to go—he handed the driver a book of matches with the logo and address of his destination.

The cab made a U-turn and began heading back to the Power Gym in Merida.

As the cab rolled slowly down the street, Ignacio steeled himself for a konfrontation. Traffic was dense, not because of other cars but because of pedestrians; a swap meet was in progress nearby, and the citizens of Merida loved a great bargain.

Ignacio was pensive. This was the last stop he needed to make before completing his mission, which he would do in spite of recent events. Though he no longer felt an allegiance to the Sandbox, he would nonetheless see to it that Kent Stirling was killed by a burning bullet to the brain delivered by the Viper.

The cab stopped outside the gym. Ignacio paid the cabbie, tipping him generously, and exited. Pushing past some of the bargain hunters, he entered the gym. Unlike before, he met no resistance; the two muscle-bound receptionists simply let him pass. Women in the club were immediately taken with his swagger; the men were intimidated by it. They watched as he strode across the gym floor with unparalleled calm and climbed the stairs to the executive office.

Unlike before, there was no one in the entry hallway, but it still reeked of past debauchery. He went to the door, opened it, and stepped into the office to find Ernesto and Consuela at the desk, alone, minus their additional muscle. It was obvious they hadn't expected any visitors, least of all Ignacio.

With shoulders back and head held high, Ignacio looked down his aquiline nose at Consuela and Ernesto. He coolly removed his sunglasses and slid them into his pocket. The recent violence at the nightclub appeared not to have fazed them. And indeed, it didn't. To them, if innocent bystanders happened to get in the way during a contracted hit, too bad. They didn't give a shit. That's what they got for being at the wrong place at the wrong time.

That didn't sit well with Ignacio. Truth be told, he wanted these two dead. He would have gladly wasted them right then and there if not for the fact that it would rain down tremendous heat from the Sandbox. But he knew he could be patient. Their time would come. He would choose the time and manner of their deaths. For now, he simply wanted them out of his life.

"Where have you been, Viper?" Consuela asked with mock cordiality.

Ignacio ignored her, fixing his steely eyes on Ernesto.

Ernesto was nervous, not knowing exactly what Ignacio's intentions were. But he put on a show of bravado, giving the Viper a broad, disarming smile. "Yes," he gushed, "we thought we had lost you for good, my friend."

Ignacio managed a slight but uneasy smile. The nerve of this asshole to act so cavalierly considering the tragedy of the other night's events, not to mention that the target hadn't even been taken out yet. He reached into his pants pocket and pulled out a single object which he laid on the desk before him. It was the key to the Mercedes. It was his quiet but precise way of communicating to Ernesto that they were finished.

Ernesto stared at the key, his eyes narrowing. He knew exactly what it meant. "I see," he said.

Consuela's smile dissolved into a severe scowl as she glared at Ignacio. She was pissed. "Well," she said, "it was a... pleasure working with the infamous Viper."

"Indeed," said Ernesto. "You are truly one of a kind, my friend."

Ignacio didn't acknowledge the remarks. He simply put his sunglasses back on, turned his back to them, and sauntered out of the office, closing the door behind him.

Consuela put her hand on Ernesto's shoulder. Both breathed a sigh of relief, feeling they had stared death in the face and survived. After a quiet moment, Consuela said, "No matter. This mission will be completed regardless of his involvement."

Ernesto nodded his agreement. "Indeed, my dear," he said. "With or without our deaf little friend, it will be done."

19

Ariel and Marisa Manzanero were in the bedroom of their home, packing their bags at the last minute before heading out the door on a two-week cruise. The girls had been sent to stay with their grandmother in Cancun. It was the Manzanero's twentieth anniversary, and they wanted a romantic getaway, not a family vacation.

Suddenly, they heard a frantic knocking at the front door, then the ringing of the doorbell.

"Who could that be?" asked Marisa, with a look of disbelief.

"You expecting someone?" queried Ariel, as he was just about to zip his suitcase shut.

"Of course not."

The knocking continued. Harder and faster, with extreme urgency.

"Don't worry," said Ariel. "I'll get rid of them." He quickly made his way down the stairs to the front door. Looking though the peephole, he was surprised to see Kent Stirling. He opened the door. "Kent...?"

"Ariel, I'm sorry," said Stirling, looking harried. "I tried you at the station and they said you'd left already. And just now, as I was knocking, I remembered you and Marisa are leaving for your vacation. Happy Anniversary, by the way."

"Thank you…we were just…"

"Do you have a few minutes?"

Ariel hesitated, and glanced at his watch. He didn't need some last-minute emergency to delay their trip. But this was an old friend, and he wasn't the sort who would leave one of his closest friends in a lurch. "Come in," he said. "Let's go to my office. We have about forty minutes before the cab arrives to take us to the airport."

"Who's there?" Marisa called down the stairs.

"It's me, Marisa," Stirling yelled up to her, in an apologetic tone. "Happy anniversary."

"He won't be long," Ariel added. "Finish packing and we'll go soon." With that, he led Kent down the hall to his home office. They entered, Ariel careful to close the door behind them before he sat at his desk. Stirling paced nervously in front of him. "Kent," asked Ariel, "what's wrong?"

"The nightclub shooting…"

"Yes?"

"I was there."

Ariel leaned forward, his eyes going wide. Then he thought for a moment, remembering his conversation with Stirling some time back. "That night you and Ariel were here for dinner…I told you we had a tip that something was going to happen at the Luna Azul."

"And you didn't know what it was."

Manzanero nodded.

"I was invited there, to meet a friend. And the next thing I know, bullets were flying."

Manzanero was dumbfounded. "Now you tell me this? Now, when I'm supposed to leave for two weeks…You know we've been gathering information from people who were there that night. Why didn't you come forward?"

"Because I also need information. I think someone's put out a contract out on me."

Ariel guffawed. This was too much. "Why? Who would want to—? I think maybe you watch too many crime stories on TV."

"Well…do you know who was behind it?"

Manzanero hesitated. He really shouldn't be sharing confidential information. But if it would give Stirling some peace of mind…

"Remember I said we had someone on the inside who'd given us the information about the club?" Stirling nodded. "One of the men who gave him that tip was discovered dead at the club. This dead man, he's a known associate of a couple we've had our eyes on for some time."

"A couple?"

"He was an assassin working for a husband and wife team who appear to have a double life. By day, they work as domestics for a rich couple in the Monte Cristo area. Their employers say they're the best housekeepers they've ever had. By night, they run their organization from their businesses—a restaurant and a private gym."

"Money laundering operations?"

"Probably. that and a lot more."

"Why would a couple of low-level crooks need assassins?"

"Because they're not low-level. Their separate identities allow them to gather information from both the worlds of wealth and finance and the criminal world. The assassins are hired as needed, to…make problems go away."

"Fucking sick people…"

Ariel tried to keep a smile from forming. He knew it wasn't exactly appropriate considering the circumstances. "Sick world we live in, my friend."

Stirling knew that truer words were never spoken. "Ariel, there's something else…"

"Go on."

"Olivia…"

"I heard she was assaulted. I'm sorry I wasn't at the station yesterday when you called. I'd already left to make last-minute plans with Marisa. How is she…?"

"She's holding up. We've closed the office for a week while I install some security precautions."

"This man who attacked her—what do you know about him?"

"Nothing really. He tried to rape her. My neighbor intervened, and Olivia got the attacker's gun and shot him."

"That must have been terrible for her." Manzanero shook his head. "Can you give me a description of the man?"

"I'd never seen him around there before. Looked like he might have been a biker. Long, greasy black hair. Bomber jacket. Bad teeth. Maybe forty, fifty."

"Sounds like a thug named Ladrillo. Olivia did the world a favor killing him. The couple I told you about, the housekeepers? He worked for them."

Stirling nodded. Pieces were beginning to fall into place.

Manzanero stood. "Kent, tell me the truth—your house, the nightclub, this incident with Olivia…for what reason do these people want you dead?"

Stirling shrugged. "I'm…stymied by it. I'm just a doctor…" He looked at Ariel, putting on his best look of innocence and consternation. He wasn't sure if Manzanero was buying it.

"Should I assign a couple of my men to protect you?"

"I appreciate that, but it's not necessary. We're going to disappear for a while."

"We?"

"Irina and I. We're leaving on the yacht. Gonna lay low until all this blows over. Visiting friends. Until we know what's going on, I want to keep her out of harm's way."

"Of course."

"I should go. Your taxi will be here soon."

Manzanero stepped around the desk to the office door. He sensed his friend was much more involved in recent affairs than he let on. But if it weren't for Stirling, he wouldn't have a wife to be taking on a romantic cruise. Standing at the office door, he said, "Kent, you know there's nothing I won't do for you, if I can."

Stirling gave Manzanero a reassuring smile. "I know, Ariel. I appreciate your friendship." They embraced, and Manzanero opened the office door and escorted Stirling down the hallway.

Maria was at the front door, having brought down her suitcase. Stirling gave her a disarming smile. "Marisa, you look beautiful."

Marisa hugged him and gave him a warm kiss. "Thank you, Kent."

"I wish you both the best vacation ever," he said, adding, "You two were made for each other."

Manzanero put his arm around Marisa. Both smiled at Stirling. "We'll see you soon," said Ariel.

Stirling gave them a nod, and turned to go to his car.

Marisa sensed something was off. "Ariel," she asked, "is he alright?"

"He's Kent. He'll be fine."

Stirling's BMW rolled to a stop outside Irina's apartment. He jogged up the steps and knocked. He heard a sound from inside—the clicking of her heels approaching the door was unmistakable. Even from a distance, he knew the rhythm of her walk. She opened the door, wearing a bright summer dress and a wide smile.

He gave her a passionate kiss and asked, "Ready to go?"

Nodding to the suitcase in the entryway, she said, "Get my bag?," making it sound more like a question than a command.

The BMW glided up the main highway en route to Progreso. As it came to the outskirts of the city, Stirling turned onto the main drag which connected to the beachfront. He parked his car in the rear lot of the Captain's Table restaurant. He was tight with the owner, who allowed him to park there whenever he needed a space.

Stirling and Irina grabbed their bags from the trunk and walked towards the pier where the yachts were docked. Josh Alan, standing at the front of Stirling's newly renovated yacht, the *Mexican Beauty,* waved to them. "So, what do you think?" he asked, as they got nearer.

The yacht's sleek design and tri-level structure was gorgeous, appearing brand new after all of Josh's work. Stirling was impressed; Irina was completely speechless. Stirling had told her to pack for a trip, but hadn't told her where they were going. It was to be a surprise. She hadn't expect an ocean voyage, but she loved the spontaneity of it all; it made it a more romantic gesture. Moments like this were part of the reason why she loved this man so.

"It looks amazing, Josh," said Stirling.

"I barely even recognize it," said Irina. "It's like a whole new yacht. Josh, you're an artist."

Josh blushed, moved by her compliment. "I have my moments," he shrugged.

Up on the main boulevard, a cab came to a stop outside the Vista Linda, private condominiums that could be bought or rented on a weekly basis. The more expensive ones had magnificent ocean views. The cab had been following Stirling's BMW from a discreet distance ever since it left Monte Cristo. The cabbie now removed a couple of oversized suitcases from the trunk and handed them to his passenger, who had disembarked—Ignacio.

After paying the cab driver, Ignacio made his way into the condos, where he had already reserved the penthouse suite the day before. He went through the lobby to the main desk and quickly checked in. Once he had his key, he strode to the elevator and took it up to the second floor. Exiting, he walked quickly to the door of his suite. Inside, he put his suitcases atop the bed and then stepped to the window of the living room. Below was a picture-perfect view of the ocean…and Stirling's yacht.

Josh finished giving Stirling and Irina an overview of the work he'd completed. "So where are you two lovebirds headed?" he asked.

"I'm not sure," said Irina. "Stirling said it was a surprise."

Josh gave Stirling a lopsided grin. "Just like you. My man!" He gave Stirling a high-five. "Well, wherever you're going, you two have a great time and don't do anything I couldn't do better."

Irina and Stirling laughed. "We'll keep that in mind," Stirling replied.

Ignacio retrieved his binoculars from his bags. Standing slightly hidden by the curtain, he opened the sliding glass door to the balcony and looked out at the sea. He focused the binoculars on Stirling's yacht, and zeroed in on his prey, at the bow of the *Mexican Beauty*, conversing with Irina and Josh Alan. After a hug from Irina and shaking hands with Stirling, Alan disembarked.

Ignacio watched him leave the boat as another man approached. This was Rodrigo Callin, a retired former tennis pro and friend of Stirling's from the Yucatan Country Club. Ignacio watched as Callin greeted Stirling and Irina and then, as they went below, Callin went into the cabin and started the boat's engines. Obviously, he was their hired captain. Typical, thought Ignacio—rich people never did for themselves anything they could hire out to someone else.

The yacht slowly pulled away from the dock and headed out to the open sea.

Ignacio was pleased. He was in a comfortable room, and would stay for as long as it took for Stirling to return. And by then, Ignacio would be ready. His escape would be planned. His target would be relaxed, calm, unsuspecting. And all it would take would be one shot.

Stirling would be dead.

Mission accomplished.

20

A tall, slender man in his mid-fifties, Rodrigo Callin still had the build of an athlete, with a broad chest, narrow waist, and well-muscled arms and legs. Unlike many men his age, he still had a nice head of hair, which he preferred on the long side so he could comb it back to cover his bald spot. Every few weeks, he dyed his hair dark brown, but under the blazing sun of the Yucatan, it quickly faded into a light brown/blonde that blended with the white roots that inevitably appeared at his temples and sideburns. His deep-set brown eyes always seemed to have a twinkle of mischief, which served him well with the ladies. Never married, he enjoyed playing the field, and was often seen in the company of women half his age as well as those his own age and, occasionally, older.

He loved to dress in pure white, which not only harkened back to his halcyon days on the tennis court but also contrasted well with his perpetual suntan, a bonus from the time he spent as the resident pro of the Yucatan Country Club and as a part-time yacht captain for close friends like Kent Stirling, who paid very handsomely for his company as well as his ability piloting vessels of all sizes through waters of all types.

Stirling came up the steps to the top deck of the *Mexican Beauty* as Rodrigo steered it out of the harbor at Progreso. "So Kent," said Rodrigo, "you want to give me an idea exactly where we're headed?"

"Well, I suppose the Captain does have the right to know our final destination, doesn't he?" joked Stirling, handing Rodrigo a cold beer.

"It would help."

"Just head toward Belize, Rod. The usual port of call."

"Nice." Rodrigo took a sip of beer, and added, "Does Irina know where we're going?"

"No, I wanted to make it a surprise. This whole getaway was done very spur of the moment."

"What's the occasion?"

Stirling gave a coy shrug.

"Where is she anyway?" asked Rodrigo.

"Down below, just resting in our room."

"Seriously Stirling, what's the reason for this little trip?"

Stirling smiled, and leaned in closer to Rodrigo, so he wouldn't have to speak loudly to be heard over the boat engine and the splashing waves, and said, "I'm going to ask Irina to marry me."

A broad smile spread across Rodrigo's rugged face. He didn't know very much about Stirling or his background, but had spent enough time with him to feel a bond of friendship. Kent was a straight shooter, a man who always kept his word, treated everyone well, and had a helluva backhand. He was thrilled for him. "Kent, that's fantastic. You're a lucky man. I'm really happy for you. For both of you." He gave Stirling a friendly, congratulatory hug.

"Thank you my friend," said Stirling. "I hope I don't throw her for too much of a loop. She probably won't see it coming, but that's the point."

"You couldn't have chosen a better spot in the world to propose. Belize never ceases to amaze me. I don't think I've ever been to a place with more natural scenic beauty in my life."

Stirling nodded. "I'm inclined to agree with you."

Ignacio. He knew this couldn't be. He'd seen her die. She couldn't have survived. She reached her arm out to him, invitingly, as if seeking for him to join her. His chest tightened. He felt like his very soul was being ripped from his body. He blinked rapidly, batting back tears. Wiped his eyes. And when he looked back through the binoculars again, she was gone.

Somehow, she had defied death. She had visited him, perhaps to let him know that she was at peace, waiting for him to join her. Or perhaps she meant to stir him to vengeance for her brutal and untimely death.

He was completely devastated. He forced himself not to weep. To hold the emotions in. Push them down. Let them stoke the fires of hatred for those who had killed his one true love.

Those whose souls he would send to hell.

Diego and Isela Tamayo resided in a magnificent beachfront estate nestled between the lush vegetation of the Belizean rainforests and the natural beauty of the sea. Tonight, they were hosting two dozen of their closest friends at this paradise on earth in celebration of Stirling and Irina's visit, congregated on the outdoor patio at the back of the house. The night air was warm, the breeze as soft as the ivory sand, and the gentle rolling of the surf calming.

The Belizean locals were a mixture of merchants, working professionals, and medical experts. Together, this group comprised some of the closest friends of both the Tamayos and Stirling. Everyone was seated at a long, elegant dining table, enjoying desserts ranging from fresh berries to homemade flan to Tiramisu, accompanied by cappuccinos and coffee.

Rising from his seat, Stirling clinked a fork against a glass until he had everyone's attention. "Excuse me," he said. "I have an announcement to make."

The Tamayos and all their guests fell silent. Stirling seemed uncharacteristically nervous. With all eyes upon him, he knelt on the dew-damp grass next to Irina's seat. Before he uttered the first word, she realized what was happening and tears came to her almond eyes. The assembled guests gasped and waited with bated breath for what they all now knew was coming.

"Irina Valverde," began Stirling, a slight tremor in his voice betraying his nervousness, "there are very few people in this world who know us both who haven't borne witness to what I realized the moment I met you. That you are without question an amazingly kind and generous woman with a warm and loving spirit. Since we've been together, there hasn't been a day that's gone by that I haven't thanked God for placing you in my path. The only hesitation I've had is questioning if I even deserve you..."

The onlookers remained silent. Some of the women wiped away tears. So, too, did Diego Tamayo, swept away by the emotion of the moment.

Tears began to roll down Irina's cheeks, despite the smile spreading across her face.

Taking her hands in his, Stirling continued, "But I truly believe we came together for a reason, and that is because we were meant for each other. I look into your eyes, and I see nothing but the one person in the world who has made me infinitely happy in every sense of the word since day one. So..." He paused to take a deep breath, trying to hold his own emotions in check. "...It is with my whole heart and soul, with which I have given you unconditionally all my love, that I ask you, Irina Valverde, in front of these witnesses...will you make me the luckiest, proudest, happiest man in the world by becoming my wife?"

With that, Irina broke down in a display of unabashed happiness, her eyes releasing a waterfall of joyous tears.

Reaching into his pocket, Stirling delicately took out an eye-popping canary-shaped diamond ring.

She took his face in both her hands and looked deeply into his eyes. "Yes. Yes, I will."

His eyes glistening, he tenderly slipped the ring on her finger, and they kissed deeply and passionately.

The Tamayos and their guests all burst into unanimous cheers and applause. The already festive mood now became a joyous celebration. Everyone was ecstatically happy for the lovers. It had been a long time coming for both of them. Champagne was uncorked, and as the evening progressed, there was much drinking and dancing beneath the moon and stars.

The party drew to a close in the wee hours of the morning, with the guest saying their farewells and giving well-wishes to the happy couple. Stirling and Irina were the last to leave, and after thanking their hosts for a memorable evening, Diego asked, "Lunch tomorrow?"

Stirling and Irina exchanged a glance and smiled, and Diego knew it wasn't to be. They both shook their heads. Lunch would have to wait. Diego chuckled and sent them on their way.

They strolled hand-in-hand down the beach, exchanging lovestruck looks, until they reached the *Mexican Beauty,* which seemed to have an incandescent glow in the pale blue moonlight.

Once aboard and in their cabin, time seemed to lose all meaning. Night became day and day became night as Stirling and Irina luxuriated in their adoration of each other. They spent the next two days and nights in bed, with Rodrigo occasionally leaving meals and drinks outside their quarters.

They were so engulfed in the joy of their impending nuptials that all they could do was devour one another through endless sessions of torrid, impassioned lovemaking until finally, on the third day, they emerged onto the deck of the yacht with glowing looks on their faces. Rodrigo had never seen two people so content. Stirling and Irina were happy, and they intended to stay that way forever, as man and wife.

Ignacio had spent his days and nights in the Vista Linda condominiums keeping vigil by the window, waiting and observing, anticipating the moment when the *Mexican Beauty* would arrive back to Progreso. When that day came, he would be ready. He would take his one deadly shot. The mission would be completed. Then he would collect his earnings and fulfill a more personal mission.

Staring out the window, laser focused, it was as if he had become a mythological statue waiting for the moment he would come alive—the split second when he would pull the trigger and end the life of Kent Stirling.

In his peripheral vision, he sensed a movement reflected in the glass of the balcony's sliding door. Turning around, he saw a faint shadow beneath the door of his suite. Someone standing on the other side. The door tremored slightly. Someone was knocking.

Rising from his chair, he slid the sniper rifle beneath the bed.

Approaching the door, he envisioned opening it to find Heidi, with her mischievous smile, standing there waiting for him just as she was when she came to his room at the Tropical Suites Hotel. If only it could be so…

Shaking the vision from his head, prepared for anything, he unlatched the deadbolt and opened the door.

He was stunned.

He had wished for Heidi.

He got Rosy Calderon.

21

"Hello handsome."

Rosy Calderon was hardly the guest Ignacio was expecting. He wondered about her motives. All he knew for sure was that she was a member of Ernesto and Consuela's crew, but tonight, she hardly seemed threatening. Her hair was elegantly tied up in a bun and her make-up was minimal. He thought she looked better without it; she was naturally attractive. It didn't hurt that she had a sensational body, with a narrow waist and bulging breasts, but there was a hardness to her features and an innate sadness in her eyes which suggested a history of tawdry sex and violence. A creature of habit, her mantra had always been that whatever Rosy wants, Rosy gets.

Tonight she wanted only one thing—Ignacio.

She sauntered into the suite as if she owned it, casually dropping her purse onto a sofa by the television. Ignacio carefully closed the door. Going to the window, Rosy looked out at the view of the port of Progreso Beach and turned back to face Ignacio.

"Come over here."

Ignacio hesitated, staring at her. He'd read her lips, and her body language, and knew exactly what she wanted. He approached her like a coiled snake. He wanted it, too. He longed for an escape, anything that would fill up the yawning chasm in his soul. Anything that would, even if only temporarily, focus his mind on something other than Heidi.

He walked to Rosy and planted himself in front of her.

"You know what I want," she said. The softness of the moonlight filtering through the sliding door complemented her, made her face look gauzy. Made it easier for him to imagine that she was Heidi.

He felt her fingers slide behind his belt buckle and tug him forward. And then he felt her hand on the crotch of his jeans, squeezing around his hard, aroused cock. He mirrored her actions, putting his hand beneath her skirt. She wasn't wearing panties. His fingertips glided over her pubic hair. And when he inserted his middle finger inside her, she clenched her vagina tight around it.

They kissed, lips locking, tongues entwined, and as they kissed, they undressed each other, practically tearing the clothes off one another. He yanked her tight blouse off as she ripped his shirt loose. He unclasped her bra with a deft, practiced move, and pawed it away from her breasts. Her nipples were hard. He squeezed one of her breasts and took her nipple in his mouth, lightly biting it.

Her hands quickly unbuckled his belt, unbuttoned and unzipped his jeans, and she dropped to her knees, tugging them down. She ran her hand over his boxers, feeling his steel-hard prick, and yanked them down. He stepped out of them. She teased him, tickling his balls and licking his fully-engorged shaft. Then she stood quickly and again plunged her tongue into his mouth. She kicked off her shoes.

And now they stood in the blue moonlight, both naked, two perfect bodies intertwined. He ran his hands over her tight round ass and lifted her up as she wrapped her legs around his waist.

He carried her to the bed and flung her, back first, onto it. In the darkness of the bedroom, it was even easier for Ignacio to imagine that Rosy was Heidi. But then she writhed, leering at him lasciviously, a look of pure lust in her eyes, and the illusion was broken. Well, he thought, if she wants it rough, I'm happy to oblige.

He yanked her legs apart and buried his face in her moist, pulsating snatch. He flicked his tongue around her clitoris, and she shuddered with a volcanic orgasm. He was just getting started. He hoisted himself upward, and maneuvered his rock-hard penis into her. He began thrusting hard. And she moaned and locked her ankles behind the small of his back and used her legs to pull him deeper inside. She didn't just like it rough—she liked it animalistically uninhibited.

She orgasmed again. Then she planted a kick into the middle of his chest, knocking him backwards. Before he knew it, she was atop him, grabbing his still-hard dick and holding it in place while she squatted atop it. Then she began grinding her hips against his. Ignacio rhythmically clinched his buttocks to force himself as deeply as possible into her. He felt he must be ripping her apart from the inside out, but she dug her fingernails into his shoulders and kept riding him as though he were a bucking bronco. She wouldn't stop until she felt his hot sperm spewing into her.

And when she did, Ignacio closed his eyes and gasped. And when he opened them again, he looked up to see Rosy letting her hair loose by yanking out a long hairpin, which she grabbed tightly like a knife and stabbed for Ignacio's head.

But his reflexes were fast. He caught her wrist in his tight grip, the hairpin mere millimeters from his eyeball. Another second and it would have plunged deep into his brain.

He snapped her wrist.

She screamed, and gave him a head butt that nearly broke his nose.

Ignacio had had enough. He belted her with a blow hard enough to knock her off the bed. She rolled onto all fours and was about to get to her feet when Ignacio pounced on her. His knee in her back held her glued to the floor. Before she could react, he interlocked his fingers beneath her chin and roughly yanked back, breaking her neck. She went limp.

He rose to his feet and fell back onto the bed, sitting on the edge, looking at Rosy's dead body. Panting, out of breath, he wondered why he hadn't let her kill him. He could have joined Heidi in whatever afterlife awaited them. Instead, his instincts saved his life, and his reflexes took Rosy's.

In a few hours it would be dawn. He took the spare blanket from the closet, spread it on the floor, flattened Rosy's body atop it, and rolled her up in it. He dressed in dark clothes, hoisted the dead body over his shoulder, and exited the hotel through a back stairwell.

On the street below, he tried several cars before he found one he could break into and steal, and used it to transport the body eastward to the wetlands at Sisal. He dumped Rosy there, in a marsh. If he was lucky, the crocodiles that he had spotted in the area would find it and feast on it. He felt invigorated; after several days of confinement in the hotel, it was refreshing to be out in the open, even on as gruesome an errand as this one.

He abandoned the stolen car halfway back to the hotel and, after wiping away his fingerprints, walked the rest of the way. As the sun colored the sky a gauzy pastel pink, Ignacio was back at his post, staring out at the ocean, waiting for the return of Dr. Kent Stirling.

Around 7 a.m., Ignacio spotted a familiar-looking yacht emerging from the early morning mist of the distant sea. As it came nearer, he raised his binoculars, and could just make out the *Mexican Beauty*, heading inland. It'll be over soon, he thought, and he'd be out of the country before nightfall.

The Mexican Beauty eventually glided up to the pier near where several other luxury yachts were docked. She stopped, and a speedboat was seen approaching. Rodrigo, on the deck of Stirling's yacht, gave a curt wave to the speedboat. This would be his ride, coming to pick him up from his stint as captain.

Through the binoculars, Ignacio could see that the pilot of the speedboat was an attractive brunette, probably in her 30s, with a slender figure—one of Rodrigo's girlfriends, Ignacio assumed. She could have been one of Heidi's models.

Why was he still thinking about her? This was not the time.…

Rodrigo berthed the *Mexican Beauty*, tying it off to a pier, and with a final wave, presumably to Stirling, he disembarked and stepped into the speedboat. He gave the brunette a kiss, then plopped down on a seat amidships as the speedboat took off in a wide arc and returned from whence it came.

Stirling and Irina were still on the *Mexican Beauty*. Ignacio raised his sniper rifle to his shoulder and looked through the telescopic sight. He twisted a knob to sharpen the focus. He could make out the shadowy silhouettes of two separate figures through the windows of a cabin on the top deck. He presumed one was Stirling, the other Irina. It wasn't as clear a shot as he wanted, and he didn't want to take any chance of making a mistake, so he waited. The last thing he'd want to do is injure Irina; she was not his target, and Ignacio was, above all, a professional.

With his eye on the scope, Ignacio followed the shadows around the cabin. And then they moved to the door and appeared on deck, but Irina was nearest to Ignacio, partially blocking Stirling. Stirling finally took a step forward. Ignacio followed him with the rifle, his finger on the trigger, but just as he was about to shoot, something blocked his view.

He lowered the rife and saw that another boat had come up to the pier, a 300-footer named *Lady of the Sea*. It was a lucky lady for Stirling, blocking him from Ignacio's lethal view. Ignacio waited patiently for either the *Lucky Lady* to pull out or for Stirling to appear on the dock.

Minutes ticked by. He saw a small group approach and disappear out of view on the far side of the *Lady of the Sea*. Ignacio guessed they were additional passengers. And after another ten minutes, the bigger yacht began to move out of its berth, once more exposing the *Mexican Beau-*

ty. Ignacio again put the rifle to his shoulder and peered through the sight.

The sea was calm, the yacht still. For several minutes, there was no sign of either Irina or Stirling. Had they disembarked? Had he missed them somehow? No, wait—he again caught sight of the shadowy figures in the top cabin.

A lone person emerged.

It was Irina. Alone. Smiling up at the sun, taking in a big breath. She was the embodiment of a woman in love. For a fleeting moment, Ignacio wondered who was he to take that joy away from her?

And then…

A bright flash.

A concussive shock wave hit Ignacio as though the air itself had shoved him backwards. Bits of debris rained down. A fireball and a cloud of roiling black smoke rose into the air. And for a split second, Ignacio could see the rocky bottom of the inlet as the water above it was blown outward. The hole immediately refilled with seawater, causing high waves that made all the boats at the pier rock and sway, their windows broken from the shock wave.

The *Mexican Beauty* was gone.

Blown to smithereens.

Ignacio's mind raced. He hadn't seen Irina or Stirling leave the boat. There was no way they could have survived the blast. Someone else had eliminated Stirling. Someone who wasn't as scrupulous as Ignacio. Someone who didn't care if there was collateral damage.

Ignacio instantly knew the culprit's identity.

Panicked citizens and horrified tourists were on the beach, some bleeding from wounds sustained when they were hit by shards of metal or broken boards from the explosion. Sirens wailed in the distance—emergency vehicles on the way. Good Samaritans as well curious passers-by and amateur online videographers rushed to the site.

Josh Alan, whose own boat had been nearly tipped over in the blast, came on deck and surveyed the chaos. And he saw a man in swim trunks with a broken face mask in the water. The diver appeared disoriented. Josh dove in and swam to the floundering man. As he got closer, he instantly recognized that it was his friend, Kent Stirling. He ripped away the face mask so that Stirling could breathe easier, then guided him to the pier. With Josh's help, Stirling climbed up the ladder and collapsed on the pier, stunned.

Josh came up the ladder after him. Stirling was just beginning to realize what had happened. Where his yacht had been there were now just flaming remnants. The yacht was gone. More tragically, she was gone. She'd stayed behind while he'd gone diving.

Stirling's whole body trembled. His eyes filled with tears. And then he screamed, crying out in agony. His cry could be heard across the pier. Josh put his hands on Stirling's shoulders, hoping to calm him.

Stirling put his face in his hands. Over and over, he muttered her name: "Irina…Irina…"

All Josh could do was hold his friend tightly, which he did, fighting back his own tears. Stirling buried his head in Josh's shoulder. Josh knew he needed to get Stirling away. As soon as Stirling could stand, Josh would take him back to his own boat. Away from the morbid looky-loos beginning to throng the beach, away from Coast Guard and police interrogators, and more importantly, away from any possible enemies who might still want to take him out.

The two-lane road to Progreso Beach was closed off and inbound traffic was backing up, but outbound was clear. Some inbound cars gave up waiting and made U-turns into the clear outbound lane, heading away from the center of the action. As they drove away, they passed a nondescript older model Toyota Corolla parked off on the shoulder.

A stocky man in a wetsuit came walking up the beach, heading for the Toyota. It was Ernesto, carrying a diving mask in his hand. He'd had an oxygen tank, but had elected to shove it out into the sea once it was depleted. He'd swum about a mile, and walked another quarter-mile, and was out of breath.

Consuela, inside the car, pushed the passenger door open. Ernesto climbed in. "Well," he said, catching his breath, "how was it?"

She handed him her cell phone. He tapped the screen and saw a video of the explosion. Even from a great distance, the fireball was impressive.

Consuela started the car and pulled onto the road.

The video ended. Ernesto chuckled, satisfied with himself.

He smiled at Consuela and said, "Mission accomplished."

22

Days after the explosion at Progeso, the scene remained unsettled. On the day it occurred, Coast Guard boats and local firefighters collaborated to put out the numerous small fires left in its wake, as well as the large flaming remnants of the yacht itself, which the explosion had propelled yards away, close to other yachts moored at the pier. Police questioned Josh Alan and Kent Stirling, who wished his friend Ariel Manzenaro was not still on vacation; the reception he got was chillier than he was accustomed to, as there seemed to be quite a lot of suspicious events occurring around him in the past few weeks.

Stirling was in a daze, muddling through, trying to keep as low a profile as possible. He found it difficult to accept that the woman whom he had just asked to marry him was now gone. The horror of it was surreal. The explosion had obliterated her; there was no body pulled from the water, only pieces. It sickened him to ponder it.

Stirling paid an uncomfortable visit to Irina's parents, Samuel and Victoria Valverde. Half-German and half-Spanish, Samuel had emigrated to the Yucatan almost fifty years ago and was a self-made millionaire. Victoria was from one of the founding families of Merida, a well-known benefactor among the social elite. A car accident seven years ago had left her confined to a wheelchair, and she had become agoraphobic. She could control what happened in her home. She could not control what happened beyond its doors.

Both Samuel and Victoria were respected for their charitable works and service to the community. And both had doted on their only daughter, whom they expected to carry their legacy into a new generation.

Stirling felt obligated to face them, felt he deserved whatever vitriol they would launch at him. If Irina hadn't been with him…

He met them at their home, behind a private gate and up a long drive past an immaculately manicured lawn. Plodding to the front door, he rang the doorbell. A servant opened it and escorted him to the patio. Irina's parents were stoic as they invited Stirling to sit and dismissed the servant.

He felt the weight of the universe on his shoulders. As he began to speak, tears welled in his eyes. His body shuddered from grief. He spoke of his love for their daughter, the wonderful times they had experienced, how happy she had been when he proposed to her. He ended by saying what he felt in his heart: "I'm sorry beyond words. I truly wish that… that it would have…"

Victoria cut him off. "No. Stop. In this house, we don't indulge in what could or should have happened. It's a waste. It changes nothing. I learned that after my accident. You can only accept what is, not wish for what wasn't."

Samuel nodded, agreeing. "We will grieve her for the rest of our days. So will you. But she wouldn't have wanted that grief to rule us. She was so full of vigor…if she were here, she'd encourage us to continue on."

Stirling put his face in his hands and wept, overwhelmed by the graciousness of the Valverdes. Victoria guided her wheelchair next to him and placed her hand on his shoulder. "You're a surgeon. Your mission is to save lives. You can't bring Irina back, but you can continue your work, and save the lives of others. And through that, perhaps, save yourself."

Stirling looked up at her. The Valverdes were offering him not blame, but absolution. He wiped the tears from his cheeks and gave a nod of understanding, and humble gratitude. These were extraordinary people.

They'd had an extraordinary daughter.

The men who took her from them would pay dearly.

Ignacio bided his time. He remained at the Vista Linda, awaiting confirmation of the wire transfer from the Sandbox, who were still on the hook for his time and expenses, even if he would have to forfeit the bounty for taking out Stirling, who he presumed was killed in the explosion. He should have a new assignment soon. His services were in high demand; he never had very much downtime between jobs.

He emerged from the bathroom after a cool shower, a towel wrapped around his waist. He'd had room service send up a fresh pot of coffee earlier. He poured himself a cup now and strode out onto the balcony, sipping it as he looked out to sea and the last remnants of the clean-up operation. There was still a faint odor of ash and fuel in the air, but there was rain in the forecast, which would cleanse it away. By tomorrow, everything would be back to normal. The police barricades would come down, the traffic along the road would resume, tourists and beachcombers would return and it would be as if nothing had ever happened. Before long, the tragedy would be trivia—"Remember when…"

He needed to get out. He'd spent too many days in his suite, grieving the loss of Heidi Aronson and regretting that it was not he who had ended the life of Kent Stirling. Granted, if not for Stirling, he would never have met her, but. . .she would still be alive.

He needed to walk, to get some fresh air and exercise, to clear his head. He got dressed. He'd been leaving generous tips for his hosts at the condos, and the cash in his wallet was just about depleted. So, he'd refresh it and find a little beachfront dive for lunch, and maybe sit there the rest of the day and try to drink the last memories of Heidi out of his head.

Dressed in his linen suit, Ignacio left the condominiums and stepped into the warm, humid air. He remembered seeing a travel agency a few doors down from the Vista Linda, next to a seafood restaurant and a local mini mart. He expected they would be able to facilitate a withdrawal of funds from his Swiss bank account and convert the Francs to Pesos.

After getting enough cash to see him through the week, he began walking to the seafood restaurant. After half a block, he stopped in his tracks, stunned. There was a news vendor's stall there, with both local and international papers available, their headlines facing out. The local papers featured a photo of Dr. Kent Stirling, looking haggard, surrounded by reporters and police, with the accompanying headline:

LOCAL SURGEON QUESTIONED
IN YACHT EXPLOSION

Ignacio couldn't believe it.

Stirling was alive.

He would be able to complete his assignment after all.

He purchased a newspaper and, stepping away, loitered next to a lamppost scanning the story, soaking up what scant few details there were. It would not be easy, thought Ignacio, to cover up, given that Stirling had very recently been involved in a house fire that was reportedly caused by a gas leak. That same excuse could not now be attributed to the yacht explosion; it strained credulity. The authorities seemed to be testing possible causes to satisfy the press and public curiosity, from a random act by an international terrorist to an explosive mine from a long-ago war washed ashore by recent storms.

Engrossed in the report, he hadn't noticed a commotion occurring behind him. A few local hooligans, taking advantage of the distracted local law enforcement, had just robbed the mini-mart. People around the front of the store screamed and scattered out of the way as the gang, led by a tall, lean, awkward-looking teenager wielding a shearing knife, raced out of the store, followed by two shorter, stockier companions.

Ignacio sensed something amiss, and turned to see what was happening. As he spun around, he stepped into the path of the tall teen, who was running too fast to stop and stumbled into Ignacio. Ignacio braced his legs to keep from falling and pushed the teen away. Horrified, the boy and his companions dashed around a corner, where they most likely had a getaway driver waiting.

Ignacio saw the shocked looks on the faces of the people around him and looked down to see blood spreading over his shirt. The shearing knife, with its foot-long, inch-wide razor sharp blade, had impaled him when the boy impacted him, its blade plunging deep just under his rib cage, below his heart. Already feeling weak from the loss of blood, he dropped to his knees. An older woman knelt at his side, praying for him. A man behind her frantically dialed a number on his phone.

Ignacio looked into the gentle eyes of the older woman. She tried to comfort him as he clutched at his wound. Whipping a scarf from around her neck, she pressed it firmly against his chest to stanch the bleeding.

Ignacio's eyelids felt like weights. His eyes closed.

All went dark.

Ignacio faded in and out of consciousness. He was vaguely aware of being lifted onto a gurney and placed in an ambulance. Remembered an orderly injecting something into his arm. Then he was out, until now, his eyes fluttering open to see fluorescent light after fluorescent light passing by overhead. He was supine, being wheeled down a long hallway with blue-gowned nurses—male and female—hovering over him.

They wheeled him into a room that was cold as a morgue and lifted him onto an operating table. Over to the side, a middle-aged female doctor was conferring with a taller male col-league, whose back was to Ignacio, both in scrubs. As he stared at them, a nurse placed an anesthesia mask over Ignacio's nose and mouth.

Through his half-shrouded eyes, he could just barely read the lips of the woman. Something about coming in on such short notice…bleeding coagulated in a sensitive area near the heart…pre-existing condition…heart surgery.

The other doctor nodded and responded. The woman pulled up her surgical mask and, as the surgeon turned around, he did the same. But in the fleeting moment before his face was covered, and before the anesthesia knocked him out, Ignacio caught a glimpse of the surgeon's face, and thought he must be hallucinating.

It was the face of Kent Stirling.

23

Ignacio awoke to the rustle of the hospital room's gray curtains being suddenly thrust open by a statuesque brunette nurse. She looked mid-20s, with a bright smile that would have been perfect if not for a slight gap in her front teeth. She needed that gap, he thought; otherwise, she'd have looked *too* perfect. He saw the name tag pinned above the breast pocket of her scrubs: Raquel.

"Oh, good," she said, "you're awake."

Looking about, Ignacio surmised that he was in a private hospital room. He felt like he'd been hit by a truck. Raquel came over to him and smoothed the sheet covering his chest.

"You may feel a little nausea, Mr. Beltran, but that's normal. It'll go away soon."

Mr. Beltran. Ignacio realized that when they found him in Progreso, he was carrying the passport that identified him as Humberto Beltran, an importer from Argentina.

Ignacio signed, "Where am I?"

Realizing he was deaf, and not comprehending what he'd signed, Raquel picked up a pad and pen from a table next to Ignacio's bed and handed it to him. He scrawled "Where?" and showed it to her.

"Where are you?" she asked. He nodded. She took the pad and paper from him and wrote "Star Medica, Medina." Now it made sense to Ignacio. He'd been brought here after he was stabbed, to the most prestigious hospital in all of the Yucatan. And he knew from the dossier of his intended target that Dr. Kent Stirling was the head of the hospital's cardiovascular surgery unit.

"Can I see the surgeon?" he scribbled.

She took the pad and wrote her answer—"I'll let him know you asked."

Seeing what she wrote, he nodded.

She said very slowly, mouthing the words carefully so that he could read her lips, "You just rest. I'll be back." She left the room, and as she opened the door, he saw that he was in Room 318. Third floor. Too high to simply leap out the window in his present condition.

When she was gone, Ignacio's head lolled to the side, and he gazed out the window at the cityscape beyond. How ironic, he mused, his life saved by the man whose life he had intended to take. When he was a child and ridiculed and bullied by schoolmates for being deaf, he'd asked his mother why he had been born with this curse. She signed to him, "The Lord acts in mysterious ways." He hadn't quite believed it then, but it certainly felt so now. If there was a God, not only did he act in mysterious ways, but he also had a wicked sense of humor.

It occurred to him that the unusual circumstances would make it much easier for him to accomplish his mission. Assuming Stirling hadn't noticed him at the club, or hadn't learned about him from other sources, Ignacio could now befriend him, reel him in, gain his trust. And when Stirling least expected it, he could kill him.

With malice on his mind, he drifted back to sleep.

Ignacio was awakened some time afterward by a hand gently touching his forearm. Opening his eyes, he looked up to see the smiling face of Dr. Kent Stirling.

"Mr. Beltran," said Stirling, simultaneously signing and speaking aloud, "Nurse DelRio said you wanted to see me." Stirling's training at the Sandbox had been exhaustively extensive, including learning how to converse in sign language, which sometimes came in handy if you needed to communicate with your partner surreptitiously.

Ignacio gave a faint smile, relieved that Stirling knew how to speak with his hands. They continued their exchange exclusively in sign language. "How long was I out?" asked Ignacio.

"You were brought in yesterday. Serious stab wound. Upon examining you, it was discovered you had a blockage in your heart. We felt if it wasn't repaired, you might not survive the surgery, so I was called in."

"Will I be alright?"

"Absolutely. It helps that you keep yourself in such good physical condition."

"Except for a bad ticker."

"Your heart is much better now than it was before I operated. Soon as you're up and out of here, you'll feel stronger than ever."

"Thanks to you."

Stirling gave a smile and a curt nod. Ignacio wondered if Stirling had any inkling who he was, so he signed, "Doctor, have we met before?"

Stirling shook his head, responding, "No, my friend. I don't believe we have." Though Stirling tried his best to be professionally courteous and upbeat, Ignacio could see the pain of loss in his eyes.

"When I am well, I want to take you for a drink," signed Ignacio. "A small repayment for the invaluable gift you have given me."

Stirling again smiled and nodded, signing, "I must go, but I'll tell Nurse DelRio to bring you lunch. You must get your strength back up. Then we'll go for that drink."

Ignacio nodded his agreement, and Stirling left.

Ignacio could sense that this was a good man.

A pity he had to kill him.

Stirling now found himself living a dual life. By day, he put on his best bedside manner, treated patients at his clinic—which had now been fortified with a video surveillance and security system to rival any embassy's; all that was miss-ing was the armed guard at the door, but Lola would have to suffice—and performed his surgical duties at Star Medica. But when those duties were finished, he found himself falling into a zombie-like funk. He was having trouble sleeping, his nights split among remorse for having put Irina in danger, paranoia about when the Sandbox would strike next, and strategizing how he could strike back at them. Some part of him always knew this time might come, but he'd hoped he'd fallen off their radar and would be able to live out his life peacefully.

He had no hope of that now.

Driving back to his practice near Progreso, he pulled up in front of the building, parked, got out, and walked around to the passenger side to casually remove his bag from the seat. It was a deliberate move, one that would allow him an opportunity to glance around at his surroundings without drawing attention to what he was doing. And as he did so, he caught sight of a black Mustang with tinted windows parked across the street. He recognized it as having also been there the day before. It appeared the driver and passenger windows were rolled down—it was a hot day—and he could just make out the silhouette of the driver inside, a hard-looking man with wire-rimmed glasses and a sharp goatee who lowered what appeared to be opera glasses as Stirling glanced at him.

Stirling felt the old instincts kicking in. He'd nev-er been able to eradicate all vestiges of the training he'd received from the Sandbox, and he was now grateful for that—he needed those lethal skills more than ever to pro-tect himself from them.

He instantly sensed the man was a watcher, assigned to track his movements. And he knew how to evade him. A water delivery truck was approaching, and would soon pass between Stirling and the watcher. That's all he needed.

As the truck passed, the watcher put the opera glasses, which were like small fixed-lens binoculars that just fit the palm of his hand, back up to his eyes. The truck rolled by, and after it passed, Stirling was gone. Probably, thought the man, he'd entered the building. But he kept watch for a few more moments just in case he reappeared.

He was startled by the glass-shattering bang of a bottle being slammed and broken against the roof of the Mustang, and in the next instant felt the sharp points of the broken bottle pressing against the jugular vein of his neck. The watcher's eyes darted to his attacker's face. It was Stirling, with a merciless, icy look in his eyes. One false move, and Stirling could slit his jugular with a flick of his wrist.

"Why are you tailing me?" asked Stirling. "Who sent you?"

He thought he already knew the answer.

He was taken aback when the trembling man stuttered, "Ar...Ari... Ariel Manzanero."

Was he telling the truth?

"Who are you?" hissed Stirling.

"M…my name's Cortez. Sgt. Re...Renan Cortez."

"Police?" asked Stirling.

The watcher gave a slight nod, scared to move too much with the sharp glass pressing into his skin. "Manzanero asked me to keep an eye on y...you wh...while he was away."

"I.D.," Stirling commanded. The watcher carefully reached into his pants pocket and pulled out his leather badge wallet. Flipping it open, he held it in front of Stirling's face. Stirling looked at the badge and I.D. card. They appeared legit. And he was ready to drop his defenses; his pulse was in his throat, his heart beating like a scared rabbit's. He was almost as frightened as the watcher.

He stepped back, lowering the broken bottle from the officer's neck. Like him, his old friend Manzanero was being extra cautious. "My apologies, Sgt. Cortez," he said. "You're doing a fine job." Stirling gently patted his shoulder. "Keep up the good work."

Stirling crossed the street and went up the steps into the building housing his office.

When he was out of sight, Cortez finally breathed a sigh of relief. He still felt scared, even though the danger had passed. Closing his eyes, he concentrated on steadying his breathing, slowing it down to normal. His heart rhythm also slowed and stabilized. He was okay. The danger had passed. He could relax. He could—oh, shit! He felt a wet warmth spread over his inner thighs and pool in the seat beneath him. He sighed, embarrassed. Screw the surveillance—he needed to go change his pants.

Olivia was at her desk doing paperwork, Lola asleep on her bed, just next to Olivia on the floor, when Stirling entered. He reached down to pet Lola. Olivia looked up, pleased to see him, but still worried about him.

He caught the concern in her eyes. "Everything alright?" he asked.

"We're fine. How about you?"

Stirling just shrugged, deflecting the question with, "How many patients today?"

"Just Mrs. Gomez at one and Refugio Metri at two-thirty."

"That's good," he said, a note of resignation in his voice.

"You sure you're okay?"

He leaned forward, hands on the edge of her desk, looking down at her, feeling the weight of his tiredness. "Thought we were being watched. Turned out to be one of Ariel's cops."

"Outside?"

"Just across the street. Guess Manzanero thought I needed a guardian angel."

"Maybe he's right."

Stirling gave her a grin. "Maybe. But we've got Lola." He scratched the back of Lola's neck. Turning from the desk, he walked back to his private office. Just inside the door was a sofa that was more decorative than utilitarian, but he used it now. Without bothering to flip on the lights, he kicked off his shoes, shucked off his coat, hung it over the back of a chair in front of his desk, and laid down. He wasn't entirely sure if it was physical exhaustion or depression, but whatever the cause, he was beat.

Laying on his back, staring up at a slowly rotating ceiling fan, he felt out of sorts. On the one hand, he felt his psyche becoming tougher, harder, adjusting to the tribulations that had been thrown at him these past weeks. But on the other hand, he felt nakedly vulnerable, in mourning not only for the loss of Irina but for the loss of himself, of who he had been, of a Kent Stirling persona that was now slipping away, beyond his control to stop it. It was like he was molting, as would a crab or a lobster, shedding his old shell to replace it with a new one. And in the deep recesses of his memory, he recalled a bit of trivia: ten percent of crustaceans die during molting, waiting for their new shells to harden so they can defend themselves.

He heard the door open, and sensed Olivia kneeling and leaning forward against the sofa, at his head. Her fingertips stroked his temples and glided over his cheek to the back of his neck. She kneaded his neck muscles. He was so tense they felt like steel cables.

He gave a little moan. During the brief time that they were a couple, he enjoyed her massages, usually administered in the wee hours of the morning after they'd made love. Their attraction was immediate and mutual, as was their realization that it was unsustainable. She was, by nature, an introvert and a loner, while he was more open and gregarious. It was a pairing of opposites that worked for the short term, but wouldn't have survived the long run.

"Anything you want to talk about?" she asked quietly.

God, yes, he thought. Everything. He wanted to tell her everything. But he knew doing so would only endanger her even more than she was already. So he lied, and whispered, "No."

He rolled onto his side and she continued her massage onto his shoulders, which felt like granite slabs. But she kept at it, quietly, and as he closed his eyes and concentrated on the tactile gliding of her fingers and nails over his back, he began to relax. He needed this. The touch of someone else. The touch of someone who loved him. He'd felt it intensely with Irina, but now he'd never—

He stopped himself. That was a dangerous rabbit hole to fall into, the depths of its darkness alluring but bottomless. No. He couldn't think about that. Couldn't think about Irina. Couldn't dwell on the past. The past was dead. Like her.

A tear escaped and rolled over his cheek. Olivia noticed. She wiped it away, and leaned down to kiss his cheek, tenderly. He turned his head to gaze into her eyes. Hers were also damp with tears. She was remembering how sweet it had once been with him. Maybe…

They stared into each other's eyes for a long moment. He wanted to grab her, kiss her, pull her onto the sofa and make love to her sweet, soft body like he had in the old days. And it seemed she wanted it, too. All he'd have to do is pull her face to his and kiss her with all the love he still felt for her. Reignite the old flame.

But he didn't. And the moment passed. For now.

"Kent…" she said with a voice as soft as a feather wafting on a summer breeze, "if you need to talk, or need a hug, or need anything at all, I just want you to know…I'm here. You don't have to go through this alone."

He took her hand in his and gave it a little squeeze, and gave her a cockeyed smile. And in that moment, that simple gesture felt as intimate as any of their lovemaking ever had.

"I know," he said. "And it means the world to me."

She stood as he rose from the sofa and embraced her. Tightly. And held it for what seemed hours, though it was only a half dozen or so seconds. He gave her a peck on the lips and said, "Let's get ready for Mrs. Gomez."

Taking his white scrub jacket off a coat rack, he slipped into his shoes and headed for the examination room. She watched him go, remembered the old times with a smile, and wiped a tear from her blushing cheek.

The sun setting over Medina painted a furious swath of red, yellow, and orange streaks across the dark blue sky. From the window of Room 318, it was a magnificent sight, but Ignacio's attention was elsewhere. With the upper half of his bed slightly inclined, his eyes were glued to the television, displaying a live soccer game. Spain versus Germany. Ignacio loved soccer and understood it with a scientific degree of precision. He appreciated the prowess of superior athletes performing at the height of their physical powers. But when Dr. Stirling entered the room, Ignacio reached for the remote and flicked the TV off.

He smiled at Stirling, surprised that he actually felt genuinely uplifted by the doctor's visit. He was beginning to have second thoughts about his mission. After all, he owed Stirling his life, which was worth far more than the Sandbox had offered for Stirling's elimination. Perhaps, he thought, fate had brought them together, and if he murdered Stirling, his luck might take a dangerously precipitous decline.

Standing next to Ignacio's bed, Stirling began communicating with him in sign language, saying, "Good evening, Mr. Beltran."

"Doctor."

"You are recovering from the procedure beautifully. I'm amazed to see you doing this well, and so quickly."

"Thanks to you, Doctor. I'm forever in your debt. There is no way I can ever repay you."

"Nonsense, my friend. You owe me nothing. I'm just glad that we came to your assistance when we did. It was definitely a close call."

Ignacio smiled at the words "close call." If only Stirling knew what a close call he'd had, being in the crosshairs of Ignacio's high-powered sniper rifle.

"Mr. Beltran, may I ask you a question?"

"Call me Humberto."

"Very well, Humberto. Is there any history of heart disease in your family?"

Ignacio pondered this, looking mildly perplexed. His mother was the only parent he ever knew. His father had abandoned her when he learned she was pregnant with Ignacio. His mother was wary of men after that; she never trusted another, and instead gave her full attention to her young son, who was born deaf. Life in the northeastern city of Cordoba was a constant struggle for the both of them. They leaned and relied on each other.

One autumn, she was stricken by a severe bout of influenza. With limited economic means, it was impossible for her to get the medical care she needed, and she surrendered to the illness one September evening, dying quietly with Ignacio lying by her side. It was a blow from which he never truly recovered.

His mother meant the world to him; she was the one person who adored him unconditionally and protected him from the harsh realities of the world. When she was gone, he was essentially thrown to the wolves, his life becoming a constant struggle. Continuously bullied, he learned he must be strong, fast, and agile to protect himself. And he could do that best if he used weapons.

His heart filled with rage. His rage fueled his talent for killing. He eventually went into the army, where he was housed and fed and taught to kill even more efficiently. And once out of the service, he went pro.

With a shrug of uncertainty, he signed, "Heart disease? No, not that I can recall. Why do you ask?"

"You had severe blockage in two of your major arteries. This is why you were suffering from extreme shortness of breath when you were brought to the emergency room. The stab wound was severe and caused much blood loss, but you would have survived it. However, if we hadn't operated when we did, it's inevitable that you would have suffered a heart attack, most likely a fatal one. In a way, the stabbing saved your life."

Ignacio was still as this startling information settled in. He, too, had been in the crosshairs without knowing it.

Stirling signed, "I know this comes as a shock, but you needed to know. We've corrected the blockages, but you should be careful of putting too much strain on your heart while it is healing. You shouldn't over-exert yourself."

"As I said, I am forever in your debt and will be grateful to you always for what you have done."

"And as I said, you owe me nothing. I was only doing my duty. Get a good night's rest. I'll be back to check on you tomorrow."

Instead of signing a response, Ignacio stuck his hand out. Stirling smiled, and shook the hand whose finger almost pulled the trigger to end his life, while Ignacio shook the hand that saved his.

Leaving Ignacio's suite, Stirling walked down the hallway and stopped briefly at the nurses' station. Raquel was on break, chatting with one of her co-workers, Vanessa, a slightly younger nurse who was petite and pretty, with ice blue eyes and jet black hair.

Stirling cleared his throat in an effort to interrupt their discussion. "Good evening, Raquel."

"Hello, Doctor."

"Vanessa, how are you doing?"

"Very well, Doctor. And yourself?"

"Fine, thank you for asking...Raquel, how is Mr. Beltran in room 318 doing as far as his appetite is concerned?

"He seems to be normal. I believe he had egg whites and oatmeal for breakfast."

"And dinner?"

"He actually requested the garlic roasted chicken and tortilla soup."

"Beautiful," replied Stirling.

"He certainly is," Raquel muttered quietly under her breath.

Stirling heard the comment and was amused. Vanessa shyly turned away, embarrassed for Raquel.

Stirling said, "I suppose he is quite handsome, isn't he, Raquel?"

Timid at having been caught, Raquel blushed.

Stirling leaned in closer to her. "I expect the two of you would make a very nice looking couple…"

Raquel smiled from ear to ear.

Stirling added, "…after he's released."

And with a slight pout, Raquel sighed, "Understood."

He gave her a curt nod. "Have a nice evening, ladies," he said as he turned and walked away. Vanessa looked at Raquel and giggled.

Stirling continued on to the elevators. He still felt exhausted, and still had much on his mind, so when the door slid open he caught only a passing glimpse of the nurse who exited, but he did register something odd about her appearance—blonde streaks through her dark hair, which was tied up in a bun. He thought he knew practically the entire Star Medica staff, but this must have been a new hire. Stepping inside the elevator car, he pushed the button for the parking level, and stared downward, deep in thought.

The nurse held a tray with what appeared to be medical instruments, covered by a cloth. She strode past Raquel and Vanessa, still gossiping and laughing, and made her way up the hall.

There was only one patient she was there to see.

The one in Room 318.

24

As Stirling approached his white Corvette in the Star Medica's garage, his mind returned to the nurse he'd glimpsed exiting the elevator. His instincts nagged him, instincts that had lain dormant for several years, but had recently begun to reawaken. Something was off, they said. Ever since meeting him, he'd suspected Mr. Beltran was hiding something. And now this mysterious visitor, exiting the elevator car quickly, with a purpose.

He trotted back to the elevator and returned to the third floor. Upon exiting, he went to Vanessa, at the nurses station. "Vanessa," he said, with a hint of urgency in his voice, "did you see where that nurse went?"

"What nurse?" asked Vanessa, innocent-eyed. It was obvious she hadn't noticed the woman, but Stirling persisted.

"Black hair, with blonde streaks. She just came off the elevator as I was getting on."

"Are you sure? Bleached hair? There's no one like that here."

"Call security."

Hearing the urgency in his voice, Vanessa immediately snatched up the phone.

Stirling dashed down the hall to Room 318. The door was slightly ajar. As he burst through, he was confronted with a scene of chaos. An IV drip stand was overturned. There was one white shoe upside-down on the floor. The bed sheet was haphazardly thrown over a body whose hand stuck out from underneath it, gripping a 9mm pistol. The head of the bed and the wall behind it displayed a dripping red burst of blood and brain matter.

Stirling pulled back the sheet. Underneath was the body of a woman, the blonde streaks in her black hair now covered in blood. There was a bullet entry wound under her chin; it was the bullet's exit that had painted the wall red and instantly ended the woman's life.

But where was Mr. Beltran? He must have done this—there'd obviously been a struggle, and he must have overpowered the so-called nurse, twisting her hand up under her chin and pulling the pistol's trigger.

There was a sound of squealing tires and a blowing car horn down below. Stirling went to the window. He saw a man flinging open the door of an SUV in the intersection, yanking out the woman behind the wheel, who was putting up a losing fight. The man was in hospital slippers with an overcoat—probably stolen—over his hospital gown. It was Beltran.

Then Stirling saw a black Camaro careen around a curve. The SUV sped towards the highway. The woman ran after it, yelling. The Camaro swerved around her, barely avoiding hitting her, and began gaining on the SUV.

There was no time to lose.

Stirling dashed to the emergency exit, banging through the door and setting off an alarm. He bounded down the stairs two and three at a time. Reaching the garage, he dashed to his Corvette and leapt in. He shot out of the garage and raced towards the highway, weaving through the nighttime traffic of Montecristo. After a few minutes, he caught sight of the Camaro up ahead and the SUV beyond it.

It was a residential zone; the highway was visible in the distance, but they were still a couple of miles away. The SUV blared its horn approaching and passing through every intersection, attempting to keep the path ahead clear. Cars ahead of it pulled to the shoulder. Some stopped abruptly in the intersections, narrowly avoiding T-boning the speeding vehicles, or being T-boned by them. The

Camaro swerved around one panicking driver and traded paint with another before falling back in line behind the SUV. And Stirling continued bringing up the rear, praying there'd be no pedestrians in their path.

Nearing the onramp to the highway, the Camaro sped up and came alongside the SUV. Close behind them, Stirling could see the Camaro's passenger window glide down, and a man leaned out of it, raising a MAC-10 machine pistol and pointing it directly at Beltran's head. There was a loud spray of bullets that shattered the driver's side window. But instead of veering away, the SUV suddenly jerked to the left, ramming the Camaro and sending it careening off the on-ramp. The Camaro tumbled and flipped over several times, pancaking the roof.

The SUV tried to swerve back to the right to make the freeway entrance, but its brakes locked and it also left the pavement, crashing into the gap where the on-ramp connected with the highway. It's hood and front fenders collapsed like an accordion.

Stirling slammed on his brakes and came to a stop just behind, on the shoulder of the on-ramp. He first looked down at the Camaro, which was beginning to smoke. The smell of burnt rubber and oil permeated the air. Stirling didn't see how the car's occupants could have survived, so he immediately turned his attention to his patient.

He went to the driver's door of the SUV and tugged on the it. It was stuck. But through the broken window, he could see Beltran, stunned and groggy, behind the wheel. Beltran slowly unbuckled his seatbelt and, seeing Stirling, waved for him to stand back. Turning around in the seat, he used both feet to give the driver's door a hard kick. It flung open.

Stirling helped him out. He appeared to be unharmed, but in his weakened condition, the exertion of the chase had taken its toll. He struggled to keep his eyes open, and struggled to walk. Pulling Beltran's arm over his shoulder,

Stirling helped him back to the Corvette and got him inside. As he got him belted in, Beltran passed out.

Stirling got behind the wheel of the Corvette and pulled onto the highway. He could hear the sirens of emergency vehicles approaching, and saw their flashing lights. As he joined the traffic cruising down the highway, there was an explosion and fireball at the on-ramp.

Josh Alan had just finished dinner aboard his houseboat, with its décor of California cool fused with Miami pastels and European vintage flavors, when he heard stumbling footsteps on the deck followed by a frantic knock. He snatched up an old-fashioned belaying pin club, just in case, went to the door, and opened it to Stirling, with the arm of his semi-conscious patient and a medical bag slung over his shoulder.

"What the hell—" Alan exclaimed.

"Help me get him in, will you?" said Stirling.

Alan obliged, putting Ignacio's other arm over his shoulder and helping Stirling guide him to a sofa. They laid him flat and Stirling immediately began a quick examination. He was glad to see there were no injuries, except for some minor cuts from the shattered glass.

"Who's this?" asked Alan.

"A patient. Someone just tried to kill him. I need to hide him while I figure out who."

"Jesus, Kent. What have you got into?"

"Not sure yet. This is Humberto Beltran, according to his ID. He's recovering from heart surgery. He's not safe at the hospital."

"How do you know?"

Stirling looked directly into Alan's eyes. "I know."

Alan knew that was all the information he'd get from Stirling, and he knew better than to probe for more. To him, Stirling was a man of mystery, one with a nebulous past that he never spoke of, and the secret of their friendship was that Alan adhered to a "don't ask, don't tell" policy. The best way for him to keep a friend's secrets was not to know them in the first place. And he liked to think of himself as someone who was always there for his friends when they needed him, but this was a big ask. Was he being coerced into doing something illegal? Harboring a fugitive?

"How long will he be here?" he asked.

"A few days, maybe a week." Stirling opened his medical kit and took out a stethoscope, checking the strange man's heartbeat. "I'll bring some supplies from the clinic tomorrow. I'll keep him sedated while he's recuperating, put him on an IV drip, get some nutrients into him, get a catheter…" He saw the look on Alan's face. "Don't worry, you won't have to deal with it. I'll come around to change it."

"What about poop?"

"I'll bring some adult diapers, rubber sheets, cleaning supplies…it'll be like changing a 180 pound baby."

"You're on your own with that."

Ignacio came out of his induced coma a few days later. His brain felt foggy from the narcotics he'd been given. There was some stiffness in both his joints and his muscles from not having used them for a while, but otherwise his body felt stronger than it had post-surgery. As his eyes focused, he saw that he was being fed by an IV bag hung from a wall lamp by a bungee cord. A window nearby was cracked open, with a faint smell of brackish seawater and tar filtering in, so he must be on a boat.

His memory was hazy. He recalled being in his hospital room, a nurse entering and marching to his bed, his realization that it was Consuela, seeing the pistol in her hand, instinctively grabbing her wrist, wrestling her onto the bed, sitting astride her as he wrapped his hands around hers and shoved the pistol under her chin, the burst of blood, running down the hall, yanking a coat off a rack as he left the building, stealing the SUV, being chased, remembered bullets shattering the SUV's window…but all was hazy after that. Had he been captured?

He lifted the cover and saw that he was in a tee-shirt and boxer shorts, not his own. He felt his cheek; from the stubble, he knew he'd been out for at least a few days. He was slightly nauseous. Maybe hungry? A little dehydrated? He pulled the IV needle out of his arm and sat up. Somewhat shakily, he stood. Shuffled to the window. Looked out. He recognized the shoreline of Progreso Beach.

As the narcotic subsided, he realized that if his enemies had captured him, they'd have killed him, not restored his health. Only one person would do that. Dr. Kent Stirling.

Walking unsteadily, he made his way out of his room and down a narrow hallway to a dining area, where Stirling sat speaking to Josh Alan at a table. Alan noticed him and directed Stirling's attention to him. Stirling got up, came to Ignacio, and helped him to the table. Alan rose, poured a glass of water, and set it front of Ignacio. Ignacio gave him a little nod of thanks.

"I'll leave you two to catch up," Alan said, before stepping outside onto the deck.

Stirling signed to Ignacio. "How are you feeling?"

Ignacio responded by signing one word: "Grateful."

They sat regarding each other for a moment, Ignacio taking a long sip of water, and then Stirling continued, "Who are you?"

Ah, thought Ignacio. He knows. No need to keep up the charade of being Humberto Beltran. He could drop the façade. He knew all about Stirling. And now that he owed his life to him, perhaps he could come clean. "A friend," signed Ignacio. "Perhaps an ally."

"We'll see," replied Stirling. He asked again, "Who are you?"

"An assassin, like you."

"Who do you work for?"

"I don't know."

Stirling gave him a puzzled look. Ignacio continued, "I'm an assassin-for-hire. I only communicate with my employers by email or text. They make a deposit into my account, assign me a mark, I carry out the assignment, and then I collect the balance of my payment."

"Who is your mark?"

Ignacio looked into Stirling's eyes. He responded not with words but with a gesture. He simply pointed his index finger at Stirling and, with his thumb, mimicked cocking a pistol and shooting it.

A cold chill ran down Stirling's spine.

"I planted the bomb in your house," signed Ignacio.

His heart racing, rage flashing in his eyes, Stirling signed, "And my yacht?"

Ignacio shook his head. "I did not murder your fiancée." He knew that if he had, and admitted to it, Stirling would have leapt across the table and instantly snapped his neck.

"Who did?" asked Stirling.

"A gang run by a husband and wife team. Utterly ruthless with hired killers to do their bidding."

"Their names?"

"I only knew their first names. Ernesto and Consuela."

Stirling realized this was the couple Manzanero had warned him about.

Ignacio continued, "I killed Consuela at the hospital."

"Why were they after you?"

"Because I've sworn to kill them."

"Why?"

"Because they killed the woman I love."

Stirling froze. These words struck a chord with him.

"Ernesto and Consuela are sloppy. Instead of waiting for me to complete my assignment, they set a trap for you, inviting you to the nightclub. Their gunmen killed many innocents that night, including my love. So I turned against them. Now they want to eliminate me."

"So you need to eliminate them first."

Ignacio nodded.

Stirling continued, "It seems we have similar agendas."

"You are the target of an organization that wants to permanently silence their former associates to protect their interests. I'm the target of the amateurs they hired to supervise my actions here. It was they who killed your fiancée."

Stirling let all this sink in. It was a twisted web, but its threads led to he and Ignacio being united in their losses. The assassin and his target had a common enemy—a covert organization that destroyed their lives, for what? The best interests of the country? The common good?

Ignacio continued, "I was offered enough money to give me lifelong security. I wanted to do this job and leave this world of killing and deception. Now I know the ones who hired me will destroy me, unless I destroy them first. So, you and I—are we friends?"

Stirling wondered how close he'd come to being taken out by the man across the table, whose life was now extended thanks to the operation he performed. Was he telling the truth? Could he trust him?

His instincts, which he was learning again to trust, told him he could. He leaned across the table and put out his hand. Ignacio extended his, and they shook hands. A silent pact.

They were in this together.

Stirling stepped out onto the deck of the houseboat and walked over to Josh Alan, resting against a rail, looking out at the sea.

"Everything okay?" asked Alan.

Stirling nodded. "We'll be out of your hair in a couple of days. And now that he's able to take care of himself, I'm going to run a little errand tomorrow, so I won't be around to check on him."

"That's fine. Looks like he'll be able to wipe his own ass now."

"Just try to keep him inside, out of sight."

"I'll do my best. Where're you headed?"

"Just going to pop in on an old friend."

Uman was a familiar place to Stirling. He'd been there in the past to visit patients as well as consult with other doctors on certain diagnoses for special case individuals. But this afternoon he drove there with a specific purpose—to visit Bernie Llewelyn. If anyone could provide Stirling with the special tools he required to take on the Sandbox, it was Bernie.

Llewelyn was tinkering in his basement when a bell sounded that clanged like a school bell at recess. He checked a video monitor connected to a camera at the front door. Not quite able to make out who was there, he slipped on his eyeglasses. The man at the door turned to glance up at the camera, and Llewelyn muttered to himself, "Well, I'll be damned..." He pushed a button to admit Stirling.

Stirling heard a buzzer followed by the clicking of electronic locks releasing. He pulled on the heavy door and stepped inside. The door had an air compression unit which closed it slowly yet forcefully behind him. Stirling knew his way to the basement door, so he went there and began his descent into Llewelyn's lab.

As he entered, Llewelyn stepped over to meet him and embraced him fondly, saying, "Kent, where have you been? I thought you were making your living as a surgeon somewhere in Europe."

"I was, for a while. Greece, the island of Crete. Made a great living. Met some wonderful people. But then it just became too hot and I needed to figure out a place where I could start over and get as far removed from the grid as possible."

"And you discovered the Yucatan?"

"Yes and no."

"How do you mean?

"I actually ended up right back where I was born."

"Belize?"

Stirling nodded affirmatively. "I found my way to the Yucatan for medical conventions, joined the board of directors of a few hospitals, and started dividing my time between Merida and Belize. Even opened a small practice near Progreso."

Llewelyn seemed impressed. "Sounds like it worked out for you."

"For a while. But now it's become too hot here."

Stirling forced a smile, but rubbed a hand across his tired brow. After years spent working together as field operatives, Llewelyn could tell his old friend was under immense pressure.

"I see. And here I thought you came all this way to tell me how good-looking I still am..."

"To me, you're a sight for sore eyes."

Llewelyn nodded. He read Stirling like a book. "So you left Greece because of the Sandbox, and now the Sandbox has found you here. You know, they didn't tell us when they signed us up that it was a lifetime commitment, and that leaving early meant not just leaving, but termination—with extreme prejudice."

"No, they didn't."

"Seems like we've been either chasing after or running from these sadistic motherfuckers since the day we were recruited. So, if I help you now, you need to promise me something."

Stirling looked into Llewelyn's eyes. "Name it."

"That you'll kill each and every one of the motherfuckers. Erase them from the face of the planet, 'cause when they're permanently eradicated, the world will be a better place."

"Bernie, you still have a colorful way of expressing yourself."

"How can I help?"

"I need whatever you can give me. Your best stuff. Got anything new?"

Llewelyn smiled wickedly.

A few hours later, Stirling had four heavy duffel bags stocked with major firepower. As he zipped the last one closed, Llewelyn asked, "Where's your car?"

"I parked in the back of your place, the empty lot where the corner house is under construction. Made sure no one saw me arrive, and no one'll see me leave."

"Good man."

Llewelyn helped Stirling take the four bags up the stairs and to the back to the house. Stirling's car was just across the narrow street, hidden behind a pile of lumber in the empty lot. Taking a couple of bags each, Stirling and Llewelyn walked them across the street. When they had finished loading them into the car, Lewellyn placed a hand on his friend's shoulder.

"Kent, when this is over, find yourself a good woman and settle down. You deserve that."

Stirling's jaw flinched. It was as though a dark cloud suddenly settled over him. With quiet conviction, he said, "I tried."

Llewelyn sensed he'd poked a fresh wound. "I'm sorry, Kent."

"You're one of the few from the old days I can still trust, Bernie. Thank you."

Stirling was turning to leave when Llewelyn, as an afterthought, said, "Wait. There's one last thing I have for you."

Stirling paused. Llewelyn dug into his pocket and fumbled around for a few seconds before getting his fingers on what he was searching for. He pulled out a cigarette lighter and held it out to Stirling.

"Take this with you."

Stirling took it and examined it. Nothing special. "You know I don't smoke."

"I know, but that's no ordinary lighter. Might come in handy."

Stirling nodded. "Alright then... show me how it works."

25

The evening was cool and crisp as Stirling drove back to Progreso. The stars shone brightly, the moon was full, and while the main boulevard wasn't quite as teeming as usual, there were still scattered locals and tourists enjoying the atmosphere of the trendy bars and the late-night eateries that never closed. Like New York, Progreso was a city that never slept, and that was exactly why the locals and tourists loved it so much. The place was alive.

Stirling parked at a corner spot adjacent to Josh Alan's houseboat, which was docked right at the corner of the pier. He stepped out of his car wearing an all-black jumpsuit, like the ones he had worn in the past on covert missions for the Sandbox. Seeing him arrive, Alan came down to help him unload, Ignacio trailing behind him.

"Nice outfit," said Alan.

"Clothes make the mission," remarked Stirling, adding, "Give me a hand with these, will you?"

They lifted the bags and carried them to the dock, Stirling hoisting two of them and Alan and Ignacio with one each. Knees buckling under the weight, Alan asked, "What've you got in here? Gold bricks?"

"Just some tools."

Alan saw how the bags were almost bursting at the seams and marveled at how effortlessly Stirling toted them. "Tools," he said. "Right..."

As they reached the dock, where Alan had both his houseboat and powerboat moored, Stirling set down his bags. The others followed suit. Looking at Ignacio, who was dressed casually in jeans, tee-shirt and work boots, Stirling signed, "Are you ready?"

Ignacio nodded. Turning to Alan, Stirling said, "Josh, we're going to need your speedboat."

"For how long?"

Stirling shrugged, "A couple of days."

Josh glanced at Stirling, glanced at Ignacio, glanced at the four heavy bags between them, and wondered what they might be planning to do with his smaller boat. But then he just shook his head with a chortle, deciding it was better not to ask, and went aboard his houseboat to get the keys.

While he was gone, Stirling and Ignacio loaded the bags into the powerboat, a 30-foot cruiser with a small cabin in the bow as well as a couple of sleeping berths and an enclosed head.

Stirling's eyes locked with Ignacio's. Both were stone cold serious. They were about to embark on their mission, and it was do or die. The doctor and the assassin were now united with a single purpose. Stirling signed, "With any luck, we'll get enough of a head start on them that we can prepare once we get to Belize. If not, once we arrive, we'll need to work fast. How familiar are you with short-range demolitions?"

A knowing smirk rolled across Ignacio's face. "On a first-name basis with them," he responded.

"And light weaponry?"

"I can shoot anything with a trigger."

Stirling nodded. "The way the Sandbox operates, they'll have alternate plans and worst-case scenarios already in mind, so we have to be one step ahead of them at all times. One last question—are you afraid of heights?"

Ignacio shook his head. He appreciated the way Stirling thought through the operation. He was as meticulous a tactician as he was a surgeon. He signed, "I think this is going to be very interesting."

Alan emerged from the houseboat, keys in hand. He handed them down to Stirling, who was on board the smaller boat with Ignacio. "Just be careful. If the waters get choppy and you kick it into high gear, she has a tendency to skip and throttle."

"Thanks for the tip."

Alan was reluctant to say goodbye, worried for his friend, hoping that things would work out all right. "I suppose this is it..."

Stirling extended his hand. "Josh, I want to thank you for all your help. I really owe you." They shook firmly.

"Not even, Doc. The pleasure was mine."

Ignacio and Alan looked at one another. Alan, aware of Ignacio's deafness, said slowly and with slightly over-exaggerated lip movements, "Take care of yourself."

Ignacio signed a message. Stirling interpreted for him, telling Alan, "He said he hopes to see you again soon."

Alan nodded and said, "I hope so."

Ignacio gave Alan a salute.

And in that instant, there was a sudden violent burst of gunfire from machine gun pistols. Alan sprinted as fast as he could for the houseboat, narrowly avoiding the flying bullets.

Ernesto emerged from the shadows onto the pier, holding an M-16 machine gun grenade launcher. He fired the shell at the houseboat. It exploded in a blast that sent debris and shattered glass floating into the night sky, and sent Alan flying into the sea, the blast concussion fortuitously lifting him above the whizzing bullets streaming past him.

There was no time to waste. Stirling gunned the speedboat's engine, and he and Ignacio jetted into the open sea sooner than either had anticipated.

Ignacio took a quick look back and was relieved to see that Alan had hidden beneath the pier and was holding on to one of the jutting logs rising from the ocean beneath the dock. He was out of sight and out of harm's way.

"Josh is fine. He made it," Ignacio signed to Stirling.

A look of relief settled on Stirling's face as they sped into the night. 9mm gunfire strafed across the water but the boat quickly outdistanced it.

At the edge of the pier, Ernesto stood looking at the disappearing speedboat and lowered his weapon. The stealthy escape of Stirling and Ignacio was a blatant act of defiance. It was as if they had cheated death, and he didn't like it.

Two of his men, wielding 9mm Uzi pistols, approached him. They were young, muscular and anxious, hyped up on the excitement. One said, watching with awe as the powerboat jetted away, "Whoaaa! We're gonna need a faster boat…"

Ernesto turned his head slowly, looking at his young underling with disgust. "No," he said, "just a lighter load." He whipped out his pistol and shot the man between the eyes. He then pointed the piece at the other man, who cowered in fear.

"What about you?" hissed Ernesto. "You got anything brilliant to say?"

"No, Sir," his subordinate replied in a barely audible whisper, his state of terror having rendered him practically speechless.

Ernesto holstered the weapon and barked, "Round up the rest of the men. We're going for a ride."

"Right away, Senor Ernesto."

As the speedboat approached Belize, Stirling noted that he wasn't far from where he and Irina had celebrated on the night of their engagement. It was only a few weeks ago, but the memory was so suppressed it felt like years. They were thoughts he couldn't entertain. Not now, when he needed his senses focused and razor sharp.

The weather was cooler here than it had been in Progreso, about 70 degrees, but slightly more humid, a small storm having passed through earlier in the day. Belize was like Stirling himself, a blend of Old World and new, with a shifting identity. It had been a British colony until 1981, and after independence the official language remained English, although nearly half the population was Mestizo, of mixed Spanish and Mayan descent, and much of the other half was Creole, descendants of West and Central Africans. The country was popular with ecotourists and American drug traffickers, the latter drawn there by the ease of laundering money with the country's lax bank regulations.

While there were large population centers, much of the Caribbean coast was forestland and nature preserves. It was here that Stirling wanted to draw his enemies, to face them in a remote area where innocent lives would not be endangered. He guided the speedboat to a narrow beach beyond which was a lush tropical forest with incredibly tall palm trees. Pencils of moonlight grazed the rain-dappled Eden below.

After pulling the speedboat up to the beach and tying it off to a fallen tree, Stirling took his cell phone out of his pocket. He powered it on and tossed it into the boat, to make it easier for the Sandbox to ping the signal and get a location fix on him. Then he and Ignacio threw the heavy duffel bags over their shoulders and got to work preparing their battlefield.

A couple of hours later, Stirling and Ignacio were taking cover behind a copse of rocks and bushes among the tall trees adjacent to the sea. Stirling heard a thrumming sound and instantly knew what it was. He signed to Ignacio that helicopters were approaching, adding, "This was what I meant by alternate scenarios." Ignacio nodded. When the helicopters were almost directly overhead, Stirling gave Ignacio a hand signal to let him know.

In the sky above, three Black Hawk choppers stopped and hovered over a line of palm trees. The doors of all three opened. Two other helicopters were approaching, not far behind. From the door of each Black Hawk, a Sandbox assassin dressed entirely in black threw down a long rope to rappel into the jungle, with other assassins in the chopper waiting to follow. As the men plummeted into the forest of palm trees, they brushed against the wide fronds. Explosions obliterated them—small but powerful mines Stirling had acquired from Bernie Llewelyn which he and Ignacio had peppered through the palms, rigged to detonate the moment any type of weight brushed against them.

The resulting fireballs lit up the night sky and whooshed upward with a heat intense enough to delaminate the rotors of the Black Hawks. The helicopters crashed through the trees and exploded on impact with the ground.

The two approaching helicopters fell back and took off across the forest, undoubtedly to land and notify reinforcements. And apparently, some attackers had arrived by boat—there was a rustle in the brush and machine gun fire whizzed over the heads of Stirling and Ignacio. They each took note of the directions from which the bullets were coming and returned fire, moving stealthily across the forest, covering each other's back, maneuvering like professional soldiers. Firing with deadly precision, they dropped two more attackers.

Suddenly, an assassin leapt over a bush onto Ignacio's back and held him in a chokehold. Stirling spun and put a bullet into the man's head. The old reflexes were still there, lethal as ever.

Ignacio was at a disadvantage. Still weak and not fully recovered from his surgery, he was functioning at about eighty percent. But his eighty percent was superior to most mens' one hundred. Catching a movement from the corner of his eye, he spun and fired, taking out another attacker. But now another man jumped Stirling, appearing out of the brush and felling him with a well-placed roundhouse kick to the head that knocked Stirling into a tree trunk, stunning him.

Steven Kobrin

Before the man could inflict further damage, Ignacio leapt into his path and delivered a lightning array of punches to the killer's face and midsection, attacking all the soft areas of his body with such speed that it was almost simultaneous. The man collapsed to his knees, and Ignacio delivered a kick of his own, snapping his neck.

Ignacio put out his hand and pulled Stirling up. Stirling had a gash in his forehead, blood trickling. "You're bleeding," signed Ignacio.

"I'm fine," responded Stirling. Aside from feeling a little dazed, he was still battle ready.

They proceeded deeper into the forest and again took cover. When Stirling paused to wipe blood from his eye, Ignacio took a pack of adhesive hydrocolloid bandages from a side pocket of his duffel bag and stuck it over Stirling's wound.

They waited in the damp grass for several minutes. Ignacio scanned the horizon with long-range infrared binoculars provided by Llewelyn. He suddenly stopped, alert. With hand signals, he communicated to Stirling that there were nine gunmen approaching.

Stirling nodded. He and Ignacio quickly removed grenade belts from their duffel bags. Each belt had a half-dozen grenades attached. They primed every one. Then Stirling silently mouthed "one…two…THREE." They flung the belts as far as they could into the dark space from which the soldiers were approaching. One of the soldiers briefly fired his machine gun.

Ignacio and Stirling hugged the ground, and there was a massive explosion. As the belts hit the ground, the grenades exploded. Each one was encased with a steel covering that, when the blast occurred, splintered into a hundred steel darts. The darts shot out in all directions, ripping to shreds the nearby bushes, the leaves and bark of the trees, and the bodies of the men.

The explosion again lit up the sky like a Fourth of July celebration, leaving behind a mist of black powder smoke and blood. After a few quiet moments, Stirling and Ignacio rose to their feet. The terrain was littered with the bodies of their would-be assassins, or pieces of them.

Stirling wondered if this was the last wave of attackers. He and Ignacio began moving back towards the beach, keeping their weapons in hand and their senses alert for any danger.

But there was none. They'd made it. They'd wiped out the first wave of men the Sandbox had sent to eliminate them, buying them a little time to figure out how to get to the real targets, the men at the top of the organization who were pulling the strings. The Sandbox could always send more Indians; they had to get to the chiefs.

After a half-hour's trek, they emerged from the forest and saw the speedboat where they'd left it, still tied to the fallen tree, though the tide had risen enough to float the vessel. Ignacio quickly signed that he would go to the speedboat first and make sure it hadn't been booby-trapped in their absence. Stirling signaled that he would cover him.

Gun in hand, Ignacio dashed out from the cover of the trees and jogged to the boat. There was no gunfire, no hidden snipers. So far, so good. He grabbed the taught rope connecting the boat to the tree and gave it a good hard yank. The boat began gliding towards him. He pulled the nose up onto the sand, went to the stern, and jumped aboard. Then he walked stealthily towards the bow, looking for any intruders.

A gunman with a MAC-10 leapt up from behind the tree where the boat was tied. Stirling fired at him, hitting him in the head, but not before the gunman got off a burst of fire that struck Ignacio.

Stirling dashed to the fallen tree. He carefully looked over it to see if any other men were hiding there. He saw no one, but noticed that the bullet fire had cut through the rope. What was left of it was dragging over the beach as the outgoing tide pulled the speedboat away from shore. Stirling ran after it, wading waist-deep in the water, and managed to grab onto the portion of the rope still tied to the boat.

Meanwhile, at the rear of the vessel, Ignacio rose unsteadily to his feet. The MAC-10 barrage had grazed his temple and left him with a burning hole through his liver. He felt weak, and as he looked up at the cabin of the boat, he saw a familiar figure coming toward him. It was Ernesto, emerging with a big carving knife in his meaty hand. Ignacio saw Ernesto mouth, "This is for Consuela!" And then the rage-filled man lunged.

Even in his weakened condition, Ignacio still had quick reflexes. He sidestepped Ernesto, simultaneously grabbing the hand that held the knife. The two men struggled, Ernesto trying his damnedest to stab Ignacio, Ignacio trying his damnedest to turn the blade back on Ernesto. They did a couple of pirouettes at the bow of the boat, until, nearing the rail, Ernesto shoved Ignacio. As Ignacio lost his balance and toppled over the back of the boat, he grabbed a fistful of Ernesto's shirt, pulling him over with him.

Going hand-over-hand, Stirling pulled himself up the rope to the powerboat's stern and struggled atop it. He realized that in his efforts to get aboard, he'd lost all his weapons. Hopefully, they wouldn't be needed from here on out.

He went to the bow looking for Ignacio, but all he found were spots of blood. He'd obviously been struck, but what had happened to him? Stirling peered over the side, looking for any sign of his friend, but there was nothing. He could yell for him, but what good would that do for a deaf man?

Then he heard the unmistakable click of a gun, and an all-too-familiar voice saying, "Looking for someone?"

Stirling turned around to face Evan Young. Like Stirling, he was dressed in the black jumpsuit of a Sandbox operative.

"Evan," said Stirling, "I wondered if you'd turn up."

"Yeah, I came down with Ernesto to make sure you didn't leave here alive. Finish the job he and the Viper fucked up."

"The Viper?"

"What? You didn't know your new pal was the Viper?"

"I just know him as Ignacio."

"Well, I know him as the beast who killed a lot of my colleagues. And yours."

"And the Sandbox hired him to kill me."

"That's right. Imagine my surprise when I found out how chummy you'd become."

"Where is he?"

"Overboard. Ernesto couldn't contain himself. Had to get revenge for the Viper killing his wife. Should have used a gun."

Stirling thought this might be it—the end of the road for him. He gave Young a resigned look, and said with a tired sigh, "If I'm going to die, I'd at least like some answers. Why, Evan? You were the only one from that place that I still trusted."

"Trust will get you killed. Isn't that what we always said? And you should know that better than any of us. Irina trusted you. Look what happened."

Stirling's hands tightened on the rail of the boat. How dare this piece of shit mention her name! "You didn't answer my question. Why?"

Young smirked. "Because Gavin Weller pays remarkably well."

"And you trust him?"

"Don't play mind games with me, Stirling. This is very simple. Weller's about to finalize a deal with a Latin American telecommunications firm that'll make him a global power broker. But he was worried what would happen if some of our former assets fell into the wrong hands, what information they might spill under torture that could come back to bite him in the ass. So…they needed to be silenced. And that's my job. And you're one of the last on my list." He raised the pistol, aiming at Stirling's brow. "You're a dinosaur. Time to go extinct."

Before he could pull the trigger, there was a terrific blast off to the side of the boat. The boat lurched, and what felt like a torrent of water splashed down on Stirling and Young. That was all the distraction Stirling needed. He grabbed Young's gun arm with both hands and slammed it against the rail. The gun dropped into the drink. Young countered with a hard left-handed punch to Stirling's throat.

Stirling's gasped, but kept up a good defense. The two men fought hand-to-hand, trading blows, slipping and sliding on the deck, Young trying to gouge out Stirling's eyes, Stirling using his elbows and knees to pummel Young's midsection and groin, stomping on his instep, kicking his knees—ironically, knowing how to save a life also meant knowing how best to end one.

A tannoyed voice came over the waves: "Hands up! Prepare to be boarded!" A gunboat was approaching fast, a spotlight on its deck catching the two combatants aboard the speedboat.

As the powerboat lurched again, Stirling lost his footing. Young delivered a vicious kick to his face, nearly breaking his nose. Stirling went down. He tried to shake it off, but when he looked back up, he saw Young towering over him. Young had ripped the stern light, on a 25-inch metal pole, loose from the hull, and was now raising it like a club, about to smash Stirling's skull. But he never got the chance—a bullet ripped through his chest. Young looked surprised. Even more so when a second bullet tore through his neck. Young staggered. Stirling gave him a good hard kick, and he fell over the rail, into the sea.

Stirling was alone now on the blood-spattered deck, exhausted and aching from the beating Young had given him. He fell onto his back, looking up at the stars, his hands splayed to either side of his head. He heard the gunboat chug up alongside. Heard men boarding the powerboat. And soon there were two officers of the Merida Municipal Police, in camouflage outfits with black bullet-proof vests and carrying assault rifles, standing over him. "Over here!" shouted one. Another man strode up. It was Ariel Manzanero.

Stirling chuckled, relieved. He said, "A little out of your jurisdiction, aren't you?"

"Friendship has no jurisdiction." Ariel put his hand out to Stirling and helped him to his feet.

"Thank you," said Stirling, with sincerity.

" I owed you."

"Did you happen to find anyone else?"

Ariel nodded. "Ernesto Echeverria. Almost ran into his body as we were approaching you. Floating out there," he pointed over his shoulder. "Face down. We pulled him in and saw that his throat was slit ear-to-ear."

Good for Ignacio, thought Stirling. "No one else?" he asked.

"Should there have been?"

Stirling didn't answer.

26

Three months later Dr. Kent Stirling was in Miami. The city was intoxicating during the late summer months. The magnificent clear blue waters of the Atlantic and the beautiful white beaches made the city all the more appealing to locals and tourists alike. The days were hot and the nights were perfect, with a sensuous combination of gentle winds and clear skies.

One of the grandest luxury hotels the city had to offer was the Four Season, where tonight a special event was occurring in the Grand Ballroom—an exclusive gala in celebration of a corporate merger between one of the largest telecommunications firms in the world and the supremely well-connected industrialist and entrepreneurial genius Gavin Weller, who was the guest of honor.

Inside the ballroom were close to 500 invited guests, and one who wasn't invited—Kent Stirling, who'd managed to secure an invitation by means of a false passport and strings pulled by Ariel Manzanero. In his black slacks, form-fitting white tuxedo jacket, and black bow-tie, Stirling cut an impressive figure, the epitome of refined masculine elegance. But unlike the other guests, he was not there to socialize and make connections while filling up on hors d'oeuvres and fine liquor. He'd come to fulfill a promise.

The host of the evening's proceedings was a diminutive European gentleman in his early 60s named Pierre. He was one of the principal heads of the Latin telecommunications firm whose leading lights were gathered at the Grand Ballroom that evening to honor the merger with Weller Enterprises.

Standing at a podium in the center of the ballroom's stage and speaking into a microphone tilted up so that he almost had to stand on his tip-toes to speak into it, he welcomed the assembled guests and said, "It is with great pleasure and excitement that I present to you a man who we all know by his reputation and our admiration, a man who has succeeded time and again in the worlds of business and high finance. A man that I am proud to announce is forming an alliance with Periveaux Communications to create the most streamlined and efficient telecommunications conglomerate in the world!"

The assembled guests—men in their tuxedos, ladies in sequined gowns—all applauded. Stirling, who'd been chatting with an attractive woman at the bar who seemed ready to leave a husband that made the marital faux pas of impregnating the hired help, joined in, though his hands clapped rather less vigorously than the others.

Pierre raised his hands to quieten the attendees so he could finish his introduction. "Without further ado, it is with great honor that I call to the stage our distinguished guest of honor, Mr. Gavin Weller!" And now the entire ballroom burst into unanimous and enthusiastic applause, along with some cheers and whistles.

Weller grazed Stirling's shoulder, but paid him no mind, as he moved through the crowded ballroom and sauntered to the stage. With the majesty of a monarch, he strode up the steps and made his way to the podium, looking out at the crowd as though they were his serfs, basking in their adulation and applause. This was his night, the culmination of all he'd worked for. Nothing could spoil it. Weller motion for everyone to take their seats. They did, and the applause subsided.

"I've never been one for long speeches," said Weller. "I've managed to do fairly well throughout the years not because I have some sort of all-seeing crystal ball, but because instinctively, I've always had a strong mind for business.

And the business of telecommunications is expanding... now more than ever. So when I decided that it was time to enter into this industry, I knew that it had to be with a winner. And Periveaux Industries have demonstrated through their bold innovation and tireless hard work that they are now and will forever be one step ahead of the pack. That is why they are the best and now...”

Weller raised a glass to toast. Pierre, at the side of the stage, joined him, along with the rest of the guests, including Stirling. Weller practically shouted the end of his toast. “Now that we are combining our companies, the merger of Periveaux and Weller Enterprises will not just set the standard for the industry—we'll be the industry!”

This brought even more applause and wilder cheers.

“To Periveaux and Weller!” shouted Weller, hoisting his champagne glass high before taking a sip.

“Periveaux and Weller!” echoed the crowd, sipping from their own glasses.

Slugging back the last of his champagne, Weller said into the microphone, “Thank you everyone. Enjoy the evening!”

There was another burst of applause as Weller descended from the stage.

Weller snapped his fingers at the band, a live 21-piece swing orchestra with a female vocalist who specialized in selections from the Great American Songbook. They began playing “Come Fly With Me.” Weller approached his partner for the evening, a significantly younger brunette with pouty lips and pretty green eyes. Other couples joined them, some accomplished swing dancers, some just improvising, but all having a good time. For a big man, Weller moved with surprising fluidity and grace, dancing like someone who truly enjoyed it.

Having moved further along the bar, Stirling noticed a stunning redhead in a low-cut black gown. He flirted with her momentarily, keeping his attention fixed on Weller. But then he noticed a blonde woman at the end who bore a striking resemblance to Irina. "Excuse me," he said to the redhead, "I think I see an old friend."

Though her blonde hair and blue eyes were different from Irina's black hair and blue eyes, the woman had an equally voluptuous figure and nearly identical features. She could have been Irina's twin. Stirling extended his hand towards her, and looked at her with such love and longing in his eyes that she couldn't possibly resist him. He invited her to dance, and she followed him to the ballroom floor.

It felt good to hold a woman in his arms again, to feel the softness of her body against his and to make light, polite conversation. But it seemed they had only gotten started when the song came to an end. Stirling took a quick glance around, clocking where Weller was standing in relation to him.

And then the band launched into a ballroom tango number, a lively tune similar to Argentinian tango, but with European and American influences. Although the dance itself was more improvisational than a traditional tango, it still had formulaic elements and was a more athletic form of dancing. And Weller excelled at it, a virtual Valentino swinging his young consort around the dance floor. He danced with a smile on his face and a gleam in his eyes, keeping his attention glued to his companion.

Stirling and his newfound dance partner also joined in. There was a certain chemistry between him and the blonde woman, an unspoken connection. He was captivated by her eyes, which had the same sensuous command that was present in Irina's. But the emotion stirring inside him was borne out of more than just nostalgia for his lost love.

Stirling had to remain vigilant; the moment he'd waited for was arriving.

As they continued dancing, Weller and his companion maneuvered to the corner of the dance floor, near the bar, where the redhead was removing a cigarette from a gold case. As she put it to her lips, Stirling and the blonde danced behind her. Stirling reached into the breast pocket of his jacket and took out the cigarette lighter Bernie Llewelyn had given him. He stretched his arm out to light the redhead's cigarette. She smiled her thanks, and as the violins and horns kept up the hypnotic tango beat, he swung the blonde around and positioned himself just behind Weller.

The music was reaching a climax. Weller raised his partner's leg onto his own, leaning over her, his other hand supporting her back. Stirling casually tilted his wrist toward Weller, pointing the top of the cigarette lighter at him, and pressed a hidden button on its side. There was a puff of air. Weller kissed his companion. He felt a twinge. He didn't realize a tiny poison-tipped dart, no larger than the end of a sewing needle, had shot from the lighter deep into his neck. The venom was already spreading through his system. Weller's instinct was to rub the stinging entry spot, but he couldn't raise his arms. Couldn't cry out. Couldn't dance. His vision began to fade.

As the music reached a climax, Weller collapsed to the floor. His companion screamed, and the dancers stopped, many of them crowding around Weller, unable to comprehend what had happened. Stirling bent over Weller, whose eyes opened just long enough for him to get a blurry look at his killer.

Weller whispered, "Stir….ling…"

Stirling said nothing. He just watched the light fade from Weller's eyes. He'd completed his mission. Weller was dead.

Stirling rose and, taking the blonde's hand, pulled her to the bar. He watched as some of the guests pulled out cellphones to call for assistance. Some others shot video of Weller's lifeless body, his companion crying over him. It would bring a pretty penny when sold to Periveaux's news outlets.

At the bar, Stirling thanked the blonde for the dance. He raised her hand to his lips and kissed it gently. Then he went out the back exit. She hoped she would see him again.

Once outside the Four Seasons Hotel, Stirling felt a weight had lifted. Irinia was avenged. His fellow agents who had been hunted down and killed by The Sandbox were avenged. Ignacio was avenged. And he was still alive.

He inhaled the cool, crisp air and admired the bright neon glow of the gorgeous Miami streets ahead of him. He could have hailed a cab or a rideshare, but he felt the need to walk, to clear his head, to be among the bustle of people.

He made his way to a more isolated part of town, highlighted by a lovely park just steps away from the beach. Then the quiet was suddenly disrupted. As he was about to cross the intersection to the beach, a drunk driver who had hit the brakes too hard and too late to stop at the light went skidding through it, grazing the rear wheel of a two-seater bicycle. The driver then floored it, making a hasty getaway, but the bicycle spilled onto the sidewalk, along with the young couple riding it. Both hit the pavement hard; thankfully they both wore helmets.

Stirling immediately rushed to their assistance, kneeling beside the couple. The young man shook his head, dazed. The young woman struggled to sit up, clutching her knee and clenching her teeth in great pain.

"What's your name?" asked Stirling.

"Stacy," she said timidly.

Her boyfriend, Wade, looked on, concerned.

Stirling ran his hands over her shin and knee until he found a tender spot that made her wince.

"Sorry, Stacy" said Stirling. "Looks like you've fractured the tibia, but it's not serious. You'll be back on the bike before you know it."

"Hey, man," said Wade, "We need to get her to a hospital."

"What's your name, Sir?"

"Wade."

"No need to worry, Wade. A few days rest will do the trick." Stirling gave Stacy a smile. She felt totally safe in his presence.

"You sure?" asked Wade.

Stirling smiled and nodded.

"I'm a doctor."

COMING SOON!

KENT STIRLING RETURNS IN

The Man From Belize
SINS OF THE RAVEN

TOP SECRET

NAME: Steven Kobrin

LOCATION: California

DISTINGUISHING CHARACTERISTICS:
Love of spy novels, thrillers, action-adventure stories, and sci-fi. Also expert on spy films.

OCCUPATION:
Author of action-adventure thrillers.

CURRENT MISSION:
THE MAN FROM BELIZE

UPCOMING:
More adventures of Kent Stirling,
THE MAN FROM BELIZE

CHECK OUT OTHER GREAT READS FROM
HENRY GRAY PUBLISHING

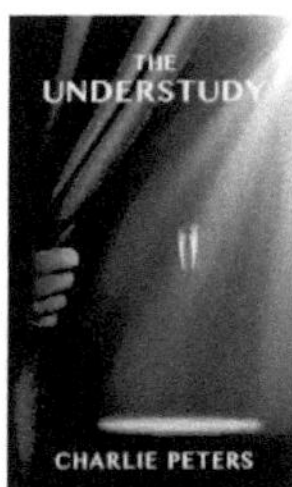

THE UNDERSTUDY by Charlie Peters

"Tell your boss that I have one of his employees."

With those words a kidnapping plot begins in the middle of a high-stakes corporate merger. But the kidnappers' plans don't unfold - they unravel.

"If you're thinking of committing the perfect crime, read Charlie Peters' **elegant new thriller** first. Find out just how many ways perfection can go wrong."—Dan Hearn, author, *Bad August*

VEIL OF SEDUCTION by Emily Dinova

1922. Lorelei Alba, a fiercely independent and ambitious woman, is determined to break into the male-dominated world of investigative journalism by doing the unimaginable – infiltrating Morning Falls Asylum, the gothic hospital to which "troublesome" women are dispatched, never to be seen again. Once there, she meets the darkly handsome and enigmatic Doctor Roman Dreugue, who claims to have found the cure for insanity. But Lorelei's instincts tell her something is terribly wrong, even as her curiosity pulls her deeper into Roman's intimate and isolated world of intrigue.

THE LAST STAGE by Bruce Scivally

Dying in his small Los Angeles bungalow, with his Jewish wife, Josephine, whom he calls Sadie, at his side, famed lawman Wyatt Earp imagines an ending more befitting a man of his reputation: returning to his mining claims in a small desert town, tying up loose ends with Sadie, and – after he strikes gold – confronting a quartet of robbers in a showdown.

For more info visit HenryGrayPublishing.com

YOU'LL FIND FUN WITH

PAPA ROCK'S WORD SEARCH *BOOKS*

PAPA ROCK'S HORROR MOVIES WORD SEARCH
by Rock Scivally

Sharpen your stakes—er, pencils—to solve these unique puzzles designed for anyone who loves classic horror films from the first Frankenstein film in 1910 to the giant bug movies of the 1950s.

If you grew up watching scary movies presented by a local horror host, or collected plastic model kits of monsters or read monster magazines, then this is the Word Search book for you!

PAPA ROCK'S SON OF HORROR MOVIES WORD SEARCH
by Rock Scivally

The 1960s. The 1970s. Two decades that encapsulated a shift in screen horror, from Dracula, Frankenstein, the Wolfman, and giant insects, to Blacula, Dr. Phibes, Regan, Damien, Carrie, a killer baby, and a rat named Ben. Pick up your pens, your pencils, or your blood-red highlighters and literally find all your horror film favorites from 1960 to 1979 within these pages. Happy Haunting!

PAPA ROCK'S ROMANCE MOVIES WORD SEARCH
by Rock Scivally and Jeffrey Breslauer

Here are Word Searches for 150 classic Romance movies made between 1921 and 1999, from the tragedy of *Camille* to the comedy of *Notting Hill*, with stops in-between for *Gone With the Wind*, *Casablanca*, *Roman Holiday*, *Breakfast at Tiffany's*, *The Way We Were*, *When Harry Met Sally*, *Jerry Maguire*, and *Titanic*, among many others. Just remember—if this book closes before you've finished working a puzzle, you'll regret it, maybe not today, maybe not tomorrow, but soon and for the rest of your life.

order yours today from HenryGrayPublishing.com